Samuel French Acti

MW01073240

American Psycho

Book by
Roberto Aguirre-Sacasa

Music and Lyrics by
Duncan Sheik

Based on the novel by
Bret Easton Ellis

SAMUELFRENCH.COM   SAMUELFRENCH.CO.UK

FOR PRODUCTION ENQUIRIES

UNITED STATES AND CANADA
Info@SamuelFrench.com
1-866-598-8449

UNITED KINGDOM AND EUROPE
Plays@SamuelFrench.co.uk
020-7255-4302

Each title is subject to availability from Samuel French, depending upon country of performance. Please be aware that *AMERICAN PSYCHO* may not be licensed by Samuel French in your territory. Professional and amateur producers should contact the nearest Samuel French office or licensing partner to verify availability.

MUSIC USE NOTE

IMPORTANT BILLING AND CREDIT REQUIREMENTS

AMERICAN PSYCHO premiered on Broadway at the Gerald Schoenfeld Theatre on April 21, 2016. The performance was directed by Rupert Goold, with scenic design by Es Devlin, costume design by Katrina Lindsay, lighting design by Justin Townsend, video design by Finn Ross, sound design by Dan Moses Schreier, and choreography by Lynne Page. The production stage manager was Arthur Gaffin. The cast was as follows:

PATRICK BATEMAN	Benjamin Walker
SVETLANA / MRS. BATEMAN / MRS. WOLFE	Alice Ripley
VIDEO STORE CLERK / SABRINA	Ericka Hunter
JEAN	Jennifer Damiano
TIM PRICE	Theo Stockman
CRAIG MCDERMOTT / TOM CRUISE	Alex Michael Stoll
DAVID VAN PATTEN	Dave Thomas Brown
LUIS CARRUTHERS	Jordan Dean
HARDBODY WAITRESS / TRAINER / CHRISTINE	Holly James
PAUL OWEN	Drew Moerlein
EVELYN WILLIAMS	Heléne Yorke
COURTNEY LAWRENCE	Morgan Weed
SEAN BATEMAN	Jason Hite
VANDEN	Krystina Alabado
AL / DETECTIVE DONALD KIMBALL	Keith Randolph Smith
VICTORIA	Anna Eilinsfeld

CHARACTERS

(in order of appearance)

PATRICK BATEMAN

SVETLANA – a Russian dry cleaner

VIDEO STORE CLERK

JEAN – Patrick's secretary

TIM PRICE – Patrick's best friend

CRAIG MCDERMOTT – co-worker, one of the foursome

DAVID VAN PATTEN – co-worker, one of the foursome

LUIS CARRUTHERS – co-worker, dating Courtney

HARDBODY WAITRESS

PAUL OWEN

EVELYN WILLIAMS – Patrick's girlfriend

COURTNEY LAWRENCE – dating Luis

SEAN BATEMAN – Patrick's brother

MRS. BATEMAN – Patrick's mother

VANDEN – club kid who sings at Tunnel

HARDBODY BARTENDER

HOMELESS MAN

HARDBODY TRAINER

CHRISTINE – a prostitute

SABRINA – another prostitute

LLOYD – Patrick's doorman

TOM CRUISE – the actor

DETECTIVE DONALD KIMBALL

VICTORIA – one of Patrick's neighbors

MRS. WOLFE – a real estate agent

OTHERS – male Wall Street-types and female hardbodies

SETTING

NYC.
Various locations, suggested minimally.
The musical moves fluidly, cinematically, and theatrically.
No transition's boring. Everything's driven by music.

TIME

1989.

MUSICAL NUMBERS

ACT ONE

"Selling Out"	Patrick, Ensemble
"Everybody Wants To Rule The World"	Patrick, Jean, Ensemble
"Cards"	Paul, Patrick, Guys
"You Are What You Wear"	Evelyn, Courtney, Women
"Happy Birthday"	Ensemble
"True Faith"	Patrick, Tim, Vanden, Ensemble
"Killing Time"	Patrick, Tim, Ensemble
"In The Air Tonight"	Prostitutes, Ensemble
"Hardbody"	Ensemble
"You Are What You Wear – Reprise 1"	Ensemble
"If We Get Married"	Evelyn, Patrick, Jean
"In The Air Tonight – Reprise"	Prostitutes
"Not A Common Man"	Patrick, Ensemble
"Mistletoe Alert"	Evelyn, Mrs. Bateman, Ensemble
"Hip To Be Square"	Patrick, Paul

ACT TWO

"Killing Spree"	Patrick, Ensemble
"Nice Thought"	Mrs. Bateman, Jean, Women
"The End Of An Island"	Evelyn, Patrick, Ensemble
"I Am Back"	Patrick, Ensemble
"You Are What You Wear – Reprise 2"	Bagheads
"A Girl Before"	Jean
"Don't You Want Me"	Ensemble
"This Is Not An Exit"	Patrick, Paul, Ensemble

ACT ONE

(An austere, clean, white apartment in New York City. Minimally decorated. A framed Man Ray print of a disassembled woman. A David Onica prominently displayed.*)

(Otherwise, whatever we need to represent the apartment and its stuff: A sectional sofa, a kitchen, a closet, a bathroom, a jukebox, a widescreen television, etc. Including a silver, chamber-like apparatus in the center of the living room.)

(We can't help but notice bloody clothes draped over a chair. A suit, a tie, a dress shirt. The red is disturbing against the white.)

(The apartment's lights start to dim and music starts to play as we hear voices coming from Patrick's TV, his stereo...)

[MUSIC NO. 00 "ON BEING PATRICK BATEMAN"]

TV, STEREO & VARIOUS. *Today computers are management tools giving you a competitive edge...*

(Then:)

Twenty-four-hour person-to-person service with every checking account...where is the nearest ATM?

(Then:)

I don't clean anymore because none of these ordinary cleaners gives me what I want...

---

*Licensees do not have rights to prints by either Man Ray or David Onica and should create original images in the style of these artists.

(Then:)

TV, STEREO & VARIOUS. ...*It took me nineteen years but I finally developed a good relationship...with my body!*

> *(The silver chamber – in fact, it's an upright tanning bed – opens slowly, revealing* **PATRICK BATEMAN**, *naked except for his tighty-whities. And Wayfarer sunglasses. Bathed in blinding white light.)*
>
> *(He steps forward, center stage. In excellent shape. In his glory.)*
>
> *(He's a rock star – a god – as he begins explaining himself and his world.)*

PATRICK. Whenever I tan, I wear a chilled, custom-made silicon gel mask to keep my eyes from looking puffy. Afterwards, I shower, using a honey-almond wash on my ripped body and an exfoliating spearmint gel on my face. I apply Clinique moisturizer before I shave – with a razor and cream by Pour Hommes. No cologne on the face, ever, as the high alcohol content dries out your skin and makes you look older...

My suit today is an eighties drape from Alan Flusser, with a bladed back to accommodate my impressive physique. My tie is by Valentino Couture; my shoes are by A. Testoni. Underwear by Ralph Lauren.

Polished, hardwood floors run throughout my apartment. The painting? A David Onica. My television? Thirty inches, digital, Toshiba. High contrast, highly defined, *plus* it has picture-in-picture capabilities, *plus*...it has freeze-frame.

> *(One more item:)*

"RONALD REAGAN" ON THE TV. *And if all else failed, you could get a sense of patriotism from the popular culture. The movies celebrated democratic values and implicitly reinforced the idea that America was special. But now we're about to enter the nineties – and some things have changed.*

(**PATRICK** *takes us into his bedroom, starts getting dressed to go out.*)

PATRICK. My Walkman, with auto-reverse continuous play, is by Sony.

(*Then:*)

I am twenty-six years old, living in New York City, at the end of the century, and this is what *being* Patrick Bateman means to me...

(*He hits play on his Walkman.*)

[MUSIC NO. 01 "SELLING OUT"]

(**PATRICK** *goes out, into the world...*)

THE STREETS ARE HUMMING
I CAN FEEL WHAT'S COMING
I SAY:

ALL.

UGH OH, UGH OH, UGH OH

PATRICK.

YOU SEE ME GLIDING
BUT THERE'S SOMETHING
HIDING IN THE

ALL.

SHADOW, SHADOW, SHADOW

PATRICK.

I MAY BE DEALING
WITH A NAMELESS FEELING

ALL.

UGH OH, UGH OH, UGH OH
BUT EVERYONE KEEPS
SAYING THAT I LOOK AMAZING
SO I
DON'T KNOW, DON'T KNOW, DON'T KNOW

PATRICK.

I WANT IT ALL!

ALL.

UGH OH, THE NEXT TRANSACTION
COME ON, SELL IT OUT

UGH OH, YOU'RE MY NEXT DISTRACTION
COME ON BABY, SELL IT OUT

> (**PATRICK** *arrives at the dry cleaners. Racks of designer clothes hanging in plastic bags.*)

> (*Perhaps* **PATRICK** *imagines a few bloody corpses, also hanging behind the counter in the plastic bags. Music underneath...*)

PATRICK. *(To audience.)* Before heading down to Wall Street, I stop at the dry cleaners around the corner from where I live – on Eighty-First Street, the American Gardens Building. The owner, Svetlana, is Russian, not Chinese, which is okay – not great – but there's *no stain* she can't erase.

SVETLANA. *(Heavy Russian accent.)* Good morning, Mr. Bateman, how are you doing?

> (**PATRICK** *gives her the bundle of bloody clothes.*)

PATRICK. Better than that fitted white linen dress shirt – can you *do* something about it?

SVETLANA. Yeah, yeah, I can clean. Tuesday okay?

PATRICK. Tuesday's *terrific*. But please, Svetlana, no bleach, okay? Bleach would *really* upset me.

SVETLANA. Yeah, yeah, I understand, no bleach –

> (*A woman,* **VICTORIA**, *comes up behind* **PATRICK**.)

VICTORIA. Patrick –

> (*He turns to her.*)

It's Victoria, from your building – well, *our* building – hi, how –?

> (*Eyeing the blood stains.*)

– Oh, my God, *what* are those stains?

PATRICK. Uhm, well, cranberry – I mean cran*apple* juice...

VICTORIA. That doesn't *look* like cranapple...

PATRICK. No, you're right, they're…Hershey's Syrup? Listen, I'm *so* late for work, Samantha –

VICTORIA. Victoria –

PATRICK. – Right. But I'll call you, Samantha, I promise –

VICTORIA. Do –

> (**PATRICK** *leaves the dry cleaners and heads back out into the city, resuming the song…*)

PATRICK.
THERE'S A RACE WE'RE RUNNING
TO THE BREAKDOWN COMING
WE SAY:

ALL.
UGH OH, UGH OH, UGH OH

PATRICK.
WE LOOK EXPENSIVE
BUT WE'RE APPREHENSIVE
'CAUSE WE

ALL.
DON'T KNOW, DON'T KNOW, DON'T KNOW

PATRICK.
DO YOU THINK I'M SAYING
WE SHOULD ALL START PRAYING?

ALL.
NO NO, NO NO, NO NO
WE'RE NOT COMPLAINING
'CAUSE THE CASH KEEPS RAINING
SO I
DON'T KNOW, DON'T KNOW, DON'T KNOW

PATRICK.
I WANT IT ALL!

ALL.
UGH OH, THE NEXT TRANSACTION
COME ON, SELL IT OUT
UGH OH, YOU'RE MY NEXT DISTRACTION
COME ON BABY, SELL IT OUT

(**PATRICK** *crosses to a video store, complete with* **CUSTOMERS** *and a* **CLERK**.)

PATRICK. *(To audience.)* It's still early, so I wander into my local video store, VideoVisions. I look for *Friday the 13th, Part Seven* – it's been awhile – but someone's checked it out. So I settle for an old favorite –

CLERK. *(Typing at her computer.)* How many nights for *A Nightmare on Elm Street*?

PATRICK. Three please.

CLERK. You sure like this movie...

PATRICK. *(Genuinely excited.)* Well, Wes Craven is an *excellent* director. And Freddy Krueger? Has become a cultural icon. Also? The scene where the blood *geysers* from Johnny Depp's bed? *The best.*

CLERK. You've rented it thirty-seven times...

PATRICK. *(Taking the movie.)* And I always find something new in it; thank you *very* much; have an *awesome* day –

(**PATRICK** *heads back out into the city, resuming the song...*)

LOOK AT HISTORY
OPEN THE BOOKS
THERE ARE STATUES WITH GREAT LOOKS
THERE ARE GODS, THERE ARE KINGS
I'M PRETTY SURE I'M THE SAME THING

BEYOND BOUNDARIES
BEYOND RULES
I'VE BEEN TAUGHT IN THE BEST SCHOOLS
THERE IS LITTLE I WON'T DO
I'M NOT LIKE YOU

IT'S HOW I'M BUILT
IT'S HOW I'M WIRED
I AM REMOTE
I AM DESIRED
I'M SOMETHING OTHER THAN
A COMMON MAN

> NO, I'M NOT A COMMON MAN
> I WANT IT ALL!

ALL.

> UGH OH, A CHAIN REACTION
> COME ON, SELL IT OUT
> UGH OH, SOME SATISFACTION
> COME ON BABY, SELL IT OUT

PATRICK. *(Arriving at:)* One last stop. The Chemical Bank on the corner of Seventy-Second and Broadway? Has an ATM that *talks* to me.

ATM. *(Speak-and-spell voice.) Good Morning, Patrick, How May I Help You?*

PATRICK. Can I get a thousand dollars in crisp fifty-dollar bills, please? My gazelleskin wallet is feeling sort of light this a.m.

ATM. *Of Course. Processing…*

PATRICK. *(To audience.)* While I wait for my cash, I notice the words "Abandon All Hope Ye Who Enter Here," scrawled in blood-red letters on the side of the Chemical Bank…

> *(While **PATRICK** speaks the above, the **ATM** does a version of the iconic "robot" breakdance. Then:)*

ATM. *Dispensing. Thank You For Your Loyalty, Patrick.*

PATRICK. No, thank *you.*

> *(**PATRICK**, in a cab, starts heading downtown…)*

> I FEEL IT IN MY HEART
> THAT IT'S ALL ABOUT TO START
> BUT I

ALL.

> DON'T KNOW, DON'T KNOW, DON'T KNOW

PATRICK.

> EVERYTHING I'M TELLING YOU'S
> A DREAM I'M SELLING YOU

ALL.

> UGH OH, UGH OH, UGH OH

(It's his final journey to Pierce and Pierce.)

PATRICK.
YOU BOUGHT IT ALL!

PATRICK.	**ENSEMBLE.**
YOU BOUGHT IT, BOUGHT IT	UGH OH, BOUGHT IT, BOUGHT IT

PATRICK & ENSEMBLE.
EVEN WHEN I WAS/WE WERE SELLING OUT

PATRICK.	**ENSEMBLE.**
YOU BOUGHT IT, BOUGHT IT	UGH OH, BOUGHT IT, BOUGHT IT
	EVEN WHEN WE WERE SELLING OUT
YOU BOUGHT IT ALL!	
YOU BOUGHT IT, BOUGHT IT	UGH OH, BOUGHT IT, BOUGHT IT

PATRICK & ENSEMBLE.
EVEN WHEN I WAS/WE WERE SELLING OUT

PATRICK.	**ENSEMBLE.**
YOU BOUGHT IT, BOUGHT IT	UGH OH, BOUGHT IT, BOUGHT IT

PATRICK & ENSEMBLE.
EVEN WHEN I WAS/WE WERE SELLING OUT

PATRICK.	**ENSEMBLE.**
YOU BOUGHT IT, BOUGHT IT	UGH OH, BOUGHT IT, BOUGHT IT

PATRICK & ENSEMBLE.
EVEN WHEN I WAS/WE WERE SELLING OUT

PATRICK.	**ENSEMBLE.**
YOU BOUGHT IT, BOUGHT IT,	UGH OH, BOUGHT IT, BOUGHT IT.

*(**PATRICK** arrives at his office.)*

[MUSIC NO. 02 "EVERYBODY WANTS TO RULE THE WORLD"]*

---

*Licensees should refer to their piano/conductor books for the lyrics to Music No. 02 "Everybody Wants To Rule The World."

*[**JEAN** and **ENSEMBLE** sing mm. 7-20 of "Everybody Wants To Rule The World."]*

*(At Pierce and Pierce, Patrick's secretary, **JEAN**, enters, approaches him.)*

PATRICK. Good morning, Jean!

JEAN. Morning, Patrick, it's late for you.

PATRICK. I had aerobics, then I was catching up on my Sally Jessy – a fascinating one-on-one with Donald Trump that I had taped – then I stopped by VideoVisions. Any messages?

JEAN. Yes. Ricky Hendricks has to cancel today. He didn't say what.

PATRICK. Boxing at the Harvard Club. What else?

JEAN. Spencer wants to meet you for a drink at Fluties Pier Seventeen, sometime after six.

PATRICK. Negative. I have plans.

JEAN. What should I tell him, exactly?

PATRICK. Just say no, Jean.

JEAN. *(Making a show of writing it down.)* "No." Got it.

PATRICK. Be a doll and get me a Perrier, okay? And *The Wall Street Journal*, and *The Financial Times*, and *The New Republic*, and –

(Suddenly remembering.)

– Wait, Jean, we haven't heard anything about the Fisher account yet, have we?

JEAN. *(Shaking her head.)* Just that it hasn't landed anywhere.

PATRICK. Okay – keep me posted, will you?

JEAN. Of course, Patrick.

PATRICK. Oh, and Jean? Don't wear that outfit again. Wear a dress, a skirt or something.

JEAN. You don't like what I'm wearing?

PATRICK. Come on. You're prettier than that.

JEAN. Thanks for the compliment, Patrick...

PATRICK. And high heels. I *like* high heels –

(As **PATRICK** *moves into formation with the other* **GUYS**, **JEAN** *sings.)*

*[***ALL** *sing mm. 29-44 of "Everybody Wants To Rule The World."]*

(The end of the song bumps us into the scene.)

TIM. *HEY! BATEMAN!* These idiots have a question for you: Is it proper to wear tasseled loafers with a business suit or not? (And don't look at me like I'm insane –)

PATRICK. You're not insane, Price, I am.

VAN PATTEN. We're sending questions in to *GQ.* We have this bet to see who gets in the Question and Answer column first.

PATRICK. You already lost, Van Patten, I was printed in their September issue.

LUIS. I admit, I'm a *GQ* virgin...

MCDERMOTT. Guys, *FOCUS*: Loafers with tassels? Yes or no? This is *important.*

PATRICK. We-*ell*, McDermott. The tasseled loafer is traditionally a casual shoe. But as long as it's black or cordovan, it's okay.

VAN PATTEN. *Ha!* See? I *told* you –

TIM. – *I* have a question for *GQ.* If all your friends are morons, is it a felony, a misdemeanor, or an act of mercy if you blow their fucking heads off with a thirty-eight magnum?

PATRICK. *(Getting the humor.)* I think that's a valid question –

(He smiles.)

– By the way, Price? You're priceless.

(Then:)

Now did you – did *any* of you assholes – read the paper this morning?

TIM. You mean *The Post*?

PATRICK. – In the same paper, the same issue – stories about strangled models; a Mafia boss thrown off a tenement building; two socialites, on a yacht, on the Hudson, *murdered* with a machete; Nazis; *neo*-Nazis; mutant alligators in the sewers; Cannibalistic Humanoid Underground Dwellers; the ozone layer *eroding*; blind mole people in the village; Kentucky-fried rats; baseball players with AIDS –

LUIS. Awful –

PATRICK. – Kids killed on subway tracks; zoo animals tortured and burned alive, *by preppies*; bridges collapsing; nuclear waste in water towers; a ritualistic murder-suicide at the Apollo; new diseases, my God, *dyslexia* –

TIM. What's your point? If you have one?

PATRICK. I don't know, Tim, maybe that *somebody* should do *something*, before we all –

MCDERMOTT. – You can get dyslexia from pussy, I heard.

TIM. No, McDermott, you can't; it's not a virus –

(Quick beat.)

Oh, shit – which reminds me. Last week, when we were at Tunnel –

PATRICK. Wait, wait, when were you guys at Tunnel? And, follow-up question, why wasn't I invited?

TIM. Calm down, you and Evelyn were at that Milli Vanilli concert at Radio City –

(Then:)

– Anyway, I pick up this Vassar chick – a tight little hardbody – I buy her a couple of champagne kirs, we're sucking face in the Chandelier Room, I take her back to my place, right?

LUIS. Go on, Tim. You're *rock*-hard –

VAN PATTEN. Hang on, where is *Meredith* through all this?

TIM. Don't be such a prude, Van Patten, I'm not buying a co-op with the girl – I'm just a guy looking for a hassle-free blow job –

LUIS. *(Trying to be included.)* Aren't we all?

TIM. – Anyway, so we're back at my place, and she's got enough champagne in her to make a *rhino* tipsy, and she *finally* agrees to give me a hand job –
(With great *meaning.)* – But get this, *she keeps her glove on.*

> *(The* **GUYS** *laugh at the absurdity of this.)*

PATRICK. Classy, Price. So – where are we having lunch? Dorsia?

TIM. Oh-you-fucking-wish. Not even *Van Patten* could get us in to Dorsia –

PATRICK. *(Strong, definitive.)* – *Fine*, but *wherever* we go, we *need* to make a reservation.

[MUSIC NO. 02A "PRE-CARDS UNDERSCORE"]

(Suddenly, the lights change and the conference room table becomes a table in a restaurant, Pastel's. A **HARDBODY WAITRESS** *delivers five Bellinis and takes their order –)*

HARDBODY WAITRESS. Welcome to Pastel's, gentlemen.

TIM. I'll have – the venison with yogurt sauce and fiddlehead ferns with mango slices.

PATRICK. The monkfish appetizer and the squid ceviche with golden caviar and...the gravlax pot pie with green tomatillo slaw.

HARDBODY WAITRESS. Delicious. Good choice.

VAN PATTEN. The scallop sausage and the grilled salmon with raspberry vinegar and a side of maple guacamole.

MCDERMOTT. I'll start with the sashimi with goat cheese and then...the smoked duck with endive and sun-dried tomato reduction.

TIM. *(Gesturing to the Bellinis.)* Yeah, and could you *please* get rid of these faggy Bellinis?

LUIS. – I'll keep mine, thank you, and nothing for me, I'm dieting, and don't look now, but *look* who just came in –

TIM. Who is that? Reed Robinson?

LUIS. No, it's Nigel Morrison –

PATRICK. That's neither Robinson, nor Morrison, that's Paul Owen.

> *(Waving him over.)*

Paul –

> *(**PAUL** starts making his way over to their table.)*

MCDERMOTT. I hear he's taking over the Fisher account...

VAN PATTEN. Confirmed. My secretary told me the same thing.

PATRICK. Fuck. So Paul got the Fisher account?

TIM. – Calm *down*, Bateman, it's a fucking *account*, not the *Shroud of Turin*...

PATRICK. *(Holding on for dear life.)* Paul Owen is wearing a cashmere one-button sports jacket and an Andrew Fezza tie, *both* impressive...

LUIS. *(Aside, to **PATRICK**.)* Do you think he has a power *jockstrap* to go along with that thing?

PATRICK. *(To audience.)* ...But it's the way he's slicked back his hair, with a part so even and sharp not even *I* could pull it off, that truly devastates me.

PAUL. Hi, fellas.

PATRICK. *(To audience.)* So I play the only card I can –

> *(Beat.)*

(To them.) Guys –

> *(**PATRICK** takes out his wallet, his new business card, and slaps it down on the conference table.)*

New card. Picked them up from the printer's yesterday. What do you think?

> *(A beam of celestial white light strikes the card. The other **GUYS** lean in. **LUIS** puts on his non-prescription glasses for a better look.)*

MCDERMOTT. Whoa.

VAN PATTEN. Very nice.

LUIS. Cool coloring... Dairy?

PATRICK. It's *bone*, Luis. And the lettering is something called...*Silian Rail*.

PAUL. It *is* very cool, but Silian Rail? Is about to be discontinued as a font.

PATRICK. *Oh, that is such bullshit –*

> *(At which point, **PAUL** slaps down his card. Again, the light, a chord of music.)*

PAUL. *Mine,* fellows –

[MUSIC NO. 03 "CARDS"]

VAN PATTEN. Holy shit –

MAGNIFICENT

MCDERMOTT.

IMPRESSIVE

LUIS.

SO THICK

TIM.

AND YET SO LIGHT

VAN PATTEN.

THE LETTERING?

PAUL.

RAMALIAN

MCDERMOTT.

THE STOCK?

PAUL.

IT'S EGGSHELL WHITE

> *(Then:)*

DON'T TAKE CHANCES IN THE GAME
IT MATTERS WHAT YOU'VE DRAWN
THE QUESTION'S NOT WHAT'S IN A NAME
BUT WHAT IT'S PRINTED ON

GUYS. *(Drums come in.)*

OH BABY BABY
YOU'RE SUCH A CARD
YOU MAKE IT OH LOOK SO EASY

WHEN I KNOW IT'S FUCKN' HARD

OH BABY BABY
THIS CAN'T BE RIGHT
HOW I LOVE YOUR SURFACES
HOW I LOVE YOUR TYPE

PAUL.

THE IMPRESSION THAT
    YOU MAKE

                PATRICK.
                HE MUST BE JOKING

IS ALWAYS IN YOUR
    HANDS

                WHAT IS HE SMOKING?

EITHER CONSTINTIA

                HE'S THE EXPERT NOW?

...OR COMIC SANS

                LIKE I SHOULD SCRAPE
                    AND BOW?

IN THE CORPORATE
    COLISEUM

                I'LL MAKE IT CLEAR

THE CROWD CALLS FOR A
    SHOWMAN

                BUT NOT RIGHT HERE

MY FONT? IMPERIAL –

                I'LL WAIT AND WATCH

YOURS? TIMES NEW
    ROMAN

                THEN TAKE HIM DOWN A
                    NOTCH

GUYS.

OH BABY BABY
YOU'RE SUCH A CARD
YOU MAKE IT LOOK OH SO EASY
WHEN I KNOW IT'S FUCKIN' HARD

    (Dance break.)

    (As the song ends, the **GUYS** *go their separate
    ways, leaving* **PATRICK** *and* **PAUL** *alone.)*

PATRICK. How...how have you been, Paul?

PAUL. Oh, terrific. Hey, how's the Hawkins account going?

PATRICK. *(Confused.)* The...? Oh, it's all right.

PAUL. And how's Cecilia? She's a terrific girl.

PATRICK. *(Shaken.)* Cecilia? Oh yes. I'm...lucky?
(To audience.) I realize, in that moment, that Paul Owen has mistaken me for Marcus Halberstam. A logical *faux pas* – *I suppose* – since Marcus and I go to the same barber at the Pierre Hotel, and Marcus *also* works at Pierce and Pierce, doing the exact same thing *I* do, but still – *I showed him my fucking card* –

PAUL. Marcus?

PATRICK. *(Quickly, hopefully.)* What are you doing tonight, Paul? Maybe we could have a drink? Catch up? Discuss things like...the Fisher account?

PAUL. Great. Yes. Let's do that. We can go to Dorsia; have you been?

PATRICK. Yes – I mean, no – I mean – I understand it's quite difficult to secure a reservation there.

PAUL. Yes, I've heard that. Tonight at eight?

PATRICK. Dorsia? Just like that? Su-ure, that would be – Fuck, no, I can't, I have –
(A thought.) Why don't you come with me? Evelyn Williams is having this dinner-party-thing at her townhouse.

PAUL. *Hmm.* Evelyn Williams is hot –

PATRICK. Is she?

PAUL. – Yeah, unfortunately, she's dating that douchebag Patrick Bateman. God, what a douchebag...

PATRICK. Yeah, what a...
(To audience, demonic smile.) – I imagine taking a serrated knife, slicing his neck open – would he *finally* stop smiling, then?

PAUL. *(Still smiling.)* Here's my card. Have your secretary call my secretary with the details, and I'll see you tonight at Evelyn's.

[MUSIC NO. 04 "YOU ARE WHAT YOU WEAR"]

(PAUL leaves PATRICK alone onstage, holding the business card.)

PATRICK. *(To audience.)* "Paul Owen's business card is nicer than mine," I am thinking. "He can get reservations at Dorsia, and I *can't*," I am thinking. "He landed the Fisher account, and I *didn't*," I am thinking. "I am twenty-six years old, and what, *what* do I have?"

(The lights shift. PATRICK exits as EVELYN and COURTNEY take over the stage, preparing for the dinner party.)

EVELYN. This is a *big* birthday for Patrick, Courtney, so thanks for being my co-host –

COURTNEY. Anything for you, Evelyn, and that outfit? To *die* for –

EVELYN. And perfectly complemented by the menu I've selected –
I WANT BLACKENED CHARRED MAHI MAHI
IT WORKS SO WELL WITH ISAAC MIZRAHI

COURTNEY.
I'LL HAVE SODA AND CRÈME DE MENTA
TASTES SO GOOD WITH OSCAR DE LA RENTA

EVELYN.
THE GINGER MANGO SOY BLACK BASS
COMPLEMENTS THE BEIGE BILL BLASS
I WILL NOT TOUCH A DROP OF RED WINE

EVELYN & COURTNEY.
DON'T WANT TO RUIN THE CALVIN KLEIN

EVELYN, COURTNEY & ENSEMBLE.
CHANEL, GAULTIER OR GIORGIO ARMANI
MOSCHINO, ALAÏA OR NORMA KAMALI
SHOULD I ROCK THE BETSY JOHNSON

OR STICK WITH CLASSIC COMME DES GARÇONS

NO PARACHUTE, OR FIORRUCCI

I'M WITH PRADA, I'M WITH GUCCI

WHEN ONE GOES SHOPPING
IT'S BEST TO TAKE CARE
AS SOME OF US KNOW
YOU ARE WHAT YOU WEAR

EVELYN.

I WILL TRY ON
THESE MAUD FRIZONS

COURTNEY.

I THINK I'D GO
TO FERRAGAMO

EVELYN.

I DON'T KNOW IF I'M SUCH A FAN
OF YOUR SPARKLY GOLD CHARLES JOURDAN

EVELYN & COURTNEY.

BUT LET'S BE CLEAR,
THERE'S NOTHING IRONIC
ABOUT OUR LOVE OF MANOLO BLAHNIK

EVELYN, COURTNEY & ENSEMBLE.

NO, THERE'S NOTHING REMOTELY IRONIC
ABOUT OUR LOVE OF MANOLO BLAHNIK

EVELYN & COURTNEY.

HUH HUH HUH HUH HUH HUH HUH

EVELYN, COURTNEY & ENSEMBLE.

CHANEL, GAULTIER OR GIORGIO ARMANI
MOSCHINO, ALAÏA OR NORMA KAMALI
SHOULD WE ROCK THE BETSY JOHNSON
OR STICK WITH CLASSIC COMME DES GARÇONS

IN A CERTAIN KIND OF NEIGHBORHOOD
YOU MIGHT GET AWAY
WITH VIVIENNE WESTWOOD

BUT BY VON FURSTENBERG WE SWEAR
IT'S A WRAP
YOU ARE WHAT YOU WEAR

> (*A spot on* **JEAN.** *A spot on* **PATRICK. EVELYN**
> *answers the phone.*)

EVELYN. This is Evelyn.

JEAN. Hi, Evelyn, I have Patrick for you?

EVELYN. Patrick! Are you getting excited, birthday boy?

(Before he can answer:)

Now listen, your brother and mother are already here, she won't take off her sunglasses, I'm worried she hates me –

PATRICK. She doesn't, she's just heavily medicated –

(Then:)

Listen, can we add Paul Owen to the mix?

EVELYN. What? Add who?

PATRICK. Paul. Owen. Read my lips. It's for work.

EVELYN. Oh, no, you are *not* screwing up my dinner party with your latest neurotic obsession –

PATRICK. He's coming, Eveyln, I already *invited* him, it's *my* birthday dinner –

EVELYN. I won't have an odd number at my table, Patrick, this isn't *Hoboken* –

PATRICK. Well – invite someone else. Can't Courtney bring Luis –

COURTNEY.	**EVELYN.**
Luis is in Phoenix on business –	Luis is unavailable –

PATRICK. For fuck's sake, Evelyn, it doesn't matter, I will bring Jean –

*(**PATRICK** "hangs up" on **EVELYN**; he and **JEAN** remain in their spots.)*

Jean, are you still on the line?

JEAN. *(Embarrassed.)* ...I am.

PATRICK. *(Bright as a penny.)* What do you say, *Jean-Jean-Jean*, I need a warm body, will you come to Evelyn's with me?

JEAN. What do I wear?

PATRICK. What you have on is...acceptable.

(The end of the song carries us into Evelyn's dinner party...)

EVELYN, COURTNEY & ENSEMBLE.
CHANEL, GAULTIER OR GIORGIO ARMANI
MOSCHINO, ALAÏA OR NORMA KAMALI
SHOULD WE ROCK THE BETSY JOHNSON
OR STICK WITH CLASSIC COMME DES GARÇONS

NO PARACHUTE, OR FIORRUCCI
I'M WITH PRADA, I'M WITH GUCCI
WHEN EVERYONE'S WATCHING, AND THE FLASH BULBS GLARE
IT'S BEST TO REMEMBER, YOU ARE WHAT YOU WEAR

(EVELYN *and* **COURTNEY** *"greet"* **PATRICK** *and* **TIM.** *The beat continues underneath...)*

PATRICK. Ladies –

COURTNEY. A bit late, aren't we, boys?

EVELYN. *(To* **COURTNEY.***)* They're *incredibly* late, in fact –
(To them.) Everyone's already here, *including* your last-minute additions, *both* of them, for which, I'm still *unbelievably* furious with you –

PATRICK. *(Ignoring* **EVELYN.***)* It's good to see you, Courtney, you look very pretty tonight. Your face has a...youthful glow.

COURTNEY. *(Touched, no sarcasm.)* You really know how to charm the ladies, Bateman, don't you?

EVELYN. *(To* **PATRICK.***)* You can ignore me all you want, but I'm *never* forgiving you –

(TIM *groans.)*

– Don't *groan*, Timothy, I wanted tonight to be perfect – not just for Patrick, but for you, too. We heard about Meredith.

TIM. – Do you have a *lint* brush, Evelyn? For my *lint*?

EVELYN. In my bedroom, you know the way. Courtney, would you get the Kirin out of the refrigerator?

COURTNEY. But of course.

(TIM and COURTNEY leave PATRICK and EVELYN...)

PATRICK. Evelyn –

EVELYN. All right, fine, I forgive you –

PATRICK. – What do you think of Paul Owen?

EVELYN. Oh, God, I don't know. He's fine, I suppose.

PATRICK. He's rich.

EVELYN. *Everybody's* rich.

PATRICK. He's good-looking.

EVELYN. *Everybody's* good-looking.

PATRICK. He has a great body. Great, uhm, definition.

EVELYN. *Everybody* has a great body now, Patrick, and I love *you*, I love *your* definition –

PATRICK. Okay, but Paul has these business cards –

EVELYN. *(Summoning the others.)* – DIN-NER!

> *(Everyone enters, assembling around the table for, truly, the dinner party from hell.* **EVELYN, COURTNEY, PATRICK, TIM, PAUL, JEAN, MRS. BATEMAN** *[elegantly dressed, pearls and black sunglasses], and* **SEAN BATEMAN** *[Patrick's younger brother, headphones and sunglasses].)*

TIM. – Get this: So far today, from the *second* I left my apartment, I've counted twenty-three homeless people. *Twenty-three* –

PAUL. *(One-upping him.)* – I've counted *thirty-four*, it's shocking –

PATRICK. *(One-upping him.)* – *I've* counted *forty-two* – and what's *really* shocking is: Most of those homeless, faceless forty-two? Most of them *want* to be out on the streets –

TIM. I call bullshit –

PATRICK. – No, no, listen, it's true. They, for whatever reason, *like* living outside – in this filthy, garbage dump of a city –

PAUL. So move.

PATRICK. *Move?* What are you *talking* about? We're in New York, where else *is* there?

PAUL. I don't know, LA? Chicago?

PATRICK. Move and do what?

EVELYN. It's a joke, he's joking, no one lives in those places – *(Offering.)* Plum wine, Mrs. Bateman?

MRS. BATEMAN. *(Like ice.)* Wine, Evelyn? From a plum? I don't think so.

JEAN. *(To EVELYN, in awe.)* Your home is beautiful.

EVELYN. *(Annoyed.)* What?

JEAN. It's so nice.

EVELYN. It's *fine.* For a struggling single girl, it's *tolerable.* But for a young, on-the-rise couple, hoping to start a family in the next year or two – well, you know I'm saying, Mrs. B–

SEAN. *(To PATRICK.)* Hey, bro – your fake tan? Is *ridiculous.*

EVELYN. Don't listen to your brother, Darling, your tan is *even* and *appropriate.*

PAUL. *(Flirting with COURTNEY and EVELYN.)* How do you two lovely ladies know each other?

EVELYN. *(Amused.)* Us? *Ooo-la-la* – Well, as a matter of fact, Kind Sir, we went to Le Rosey together –

COURTNEY. *(To JEAN.)* That's in Switzerland –

EVELYN. – Then business school in Geneva –

COURTNEY. – Also in Switzerland –

EVELYN. – I barely scraped through, but Courtney, upon graduation, was aggressively recruited by *many* headhunters, she's smarter than anyone else at this table –

COURTNEY. *(Light, carefree.)* – Which is why I drink and do lithium.

PATRICK. *(Ignoring the women; fixated on:)* Where'd *you* go to school, Paul?

TIM. Oh, for Christ's sake – Just suck his dick, will you?

PAUL. Harvard –

PATRICK. *(Hah!)* Me, too –

PAUL. Then the London School of Economics.

PATRICK. *(Fuck you.) Fuck you* –

EVELYN. – *Sean*, you were telling me about some article you were working on? For that literary journal? What was it about?

SEAN. The Death of Downtown.

PATRICK. *(Coughing, under his breath.)* Get a job.

PAUL. That sounds like a cool topic. I should definitely check that out.

PATRICK. Why? No one gives a rat's ass about the Death of Downtown –

JEAN. Actually, *I* live downtown –

PAUL. Yes, and there are some really cool clubs south of Twentieth – Danceteria – so, hey, if downtown's dying, *I* care.

PATRICK. About a couple of bars closing? What about current events, huh? What about, like, apartheid?

PAUL. What *about* it?

PATRICK. Well – we have to end it, for one! And not just apartheid,

[MUSIC NO. 05 "HAPPY BIRTHDAY"]

the nuclear arms race –

TIM. *(Instigating.) Go on.*

PATRICK. We have to slow it down, obviously – And, and stop terrorism – *as well as* world hunger –

MRS. BATEMAN. Is anyone else starving?

PATRICK. At which point, I would shore up our national defense – all the while curbing the spread of communism in Central America – as well as work toward a Middle East peace settlement –

PAUL. That would be good –

PATRICK. We have to – *have to* – decrease U.S. military involvement overseas, if not prevent it altogether –

EVELYN. Are we forgetting why we're here?

(*Sing-songy.*) It's somebody's birthday –

> (**EVELYN** *gestures to* **COURTNEY**, *who exits.*)

PATRICK. Domestically – we're in trouble. We need affordable health-care for the elderly – Also: *Why* is it *so hard* to control and find a cure for AIDS?

EVELYN. *AIDS?! Not at the dinner table –*

PATRICK. (*On a roll.*) Let's crack down on crime and illegal drugs, *especially* cocaine – protect Social Security – We need to stop people from abusing the welfare system – oppose racial discrimination – promote civil rights, while at the same time promoting equal rights for women –

EVELYN. (*Annoyed.*) Thanks for that –

PATRICK. The abortion laws *have* to change – to protect the right to life – while somehow *maintaining* women's freedom of choice – What else? Illegal immigrants?

EVELYN. *PATRICK –*

> (*He stares at* **EVELYN**, *as behind him* **COURTNEY**, *carrying a big birthday cake with twenty-seven lit candles, enters with the* **FOUR WAITRESSES**.)

MRS. BATEMAN. It's your favorite, darling. Red velvet.

FOUR WAITRESSES.

HAPPY BIRTHDAY TO YOU

HAPPY BIRTHDAY TO YOU

HAPPY BIRTHDAY PATRICK BATEMAN

HAPPY BIRTHDAY TO YOU –

MRS. BATEMAN.

HOW OLD ARE YOU?

SEAN.

HOW OLD ARE YOU?

EVELYN & COURTNEY.

HOW OLD, HOW OLD

TIM.

HOW OLD ARE YOU?

*(**COURTNEY** has placed the cake on the table in front of **PATRICK**. Beat of silence.)*

PATRICK. *(A dread-filled realization.)* I'm twenty-seven years old today...

PAUL. Blow out the candles, Marcus.

*(**PATRICK** slowly turns to **PAUL**, shaking with internal rage...)*

PATRICK. *(To audience.)* I am a ghost to these people...

PAUL. Make a wish.

PATRICK. I wish to fit in...

*(Beat...then **PATRICK** suddenly whips back to the cake and blows out the candles in a King Lear-like rage, violently.)*

EVELYN. Did you *have* to spit? And Courtney, you forgot the knife –

*(But **PATRICK** reaches into his jacket pocket –)*

PATRICK. I have one –

(– And pulls out a terrifying butcher knife. Beat, then he starts hacking into the cake, violently, decimating it.)

*(Everyone's in silent shock; he doesn't stop until **JEAN** says:)*

JEAN. *PATRICK* –

*(He stops, but it's too late. A moment of quiet – and real – hurt for **EVELYN**. Then, the wall goes up again.)*

EVELYN. *(Brightly.)* Palate-cleansing sorbet in the kitchen? I have an assortment: Kiwi, carambola, cherimoya, Japanese pear, and cactus fruit. Everyone, follow me –

*(They all stand to go with her, including **PATRICK** –)*

Not you, you're banished –

PATRICK. Evelyn –

EVELYN. Don't even *think* about calling me for the next twenty-four to thirty-six hours, Mr. Bateman –

> *(Everyone exits except for* **PATRICK** *and* **TIM** *and maybe one of the* **WAITRESSES**.*)*

TIM. *(To* **WAITRESS**.*)* Hey, can I get your number? *Whatever* –

(To **PATRICK**.*)* It's still early, pal – you wanna hit the clubs? Maybe start with Tunnel?

(Before **PATRICK** *can answer.)* – Yeah, you do –

> *(Turning, he spots a cab.)*

TAXI –

> *(The lights change, hard and fast.* **PATRICK** *and* **TIM**, *in the back seat of a cab.)*

PATRICK. – Jesus-fucking-Christ, this moron fucking-cabbie – Not the *Lincoln* Tunnel, not the *Holland* Tunnel, the club *Tunnel*, it's in *Chelsea*, on *Eleventh* Avenue –

> **(TIM** *is searching his jacket pockets –)*

TIM. – Hey, so I dumped Meredith, did I tell you? She's been essentially *daring* me to like her, right? So fuck that, I'm gone. I mean, I tell her I'm sensitive –

PATRICK. You are; you were...

> *(Grasping for it.)*

– very freaked out by the Challenger accident, I remember –

TIM. I mean, what more does she want?

PATRICK. *(To audience, urgent.)* – The Hudson River races past us. Dark, eternal, an abyss. It's the River Styx tonight, and I –

(To **CABBIE**.*)* GODDAMMIT, FASTER – GO – FASTER – *(Under his breath.)* Asshole –

TIM. You're freaking me out, Bateman, what is it – steroids? I thought you were off them –

PATRICK. – I *am* off them, Price –

(Shaking his head.)

No, it's *not* the steroids, it's...

(Struggling to make sense of it.)

...The world – everything – out there – rushing by –

TIM. *(Meaning "it's okay.")* We'll get to Tunnel, we'll get shit-faced, it'll be *fine* –

PATRICK. – Will it?

(Beat, then:)

There are these...tracks in the dance floor at Tunnel. Why the hell are there train tracks in the dance floor?

TIM. They're from the past.

PATRICK. What do you mean, the past?

TIM. *(To **CABBIE**.)* Oh, we're here – On the right, pull –

PATRICK. *(Yelling.)* PULL – THE FUCK – OVER – *(Asshole –)*

(We're at Tunnel.)

[MUSIC NO. 06 "TRUE FAITH"]*

TIM. ...Hang tight. Lemme talk to the bouncer.

*(**TIM** steps away from **PATRICK**.)*

PATRICK. *(Nodding, to audience.)* – *Whatever* existential horror is building within me, and I can feel it, I can feel it coming on, when we get to Tunnel, a song I love is spilling *out* of the club, *onto* the sidewalk, filling me with this strange, sudden desire to...

(A shift here.)

...*chill*. To get in there, drink some champagne, flirt with a hardbody, find some blow, and maybe...even... dance...

*(**PATRICK** and the ensemble **MEN** and **WOMEN** start dancing wild to "True Faith." **VANDEN**, a club kid, welcomes us –)*

*[**VANDEN** and **ENSEMBLE** sing "True Faith."]*

---

*Licensees should refer to their piano/conductor books for the lyrics to Music No. 06 "True Faith."

*(The rest of "True Faith" happens under the following scene. **TIM** goes one way, but we follow **PATRICK** as he approaches the bar.)*

PATRICK. *(To **HARDBODY BARTENDER**.)* Hey, can I get two double Stolis on the rocks?

*(**PATRICK** lays down a twenty.)*

HARDBODY BARTENDER. Coming right up.

PATRICK. *(As she fixes the drinks.)* Wait, didn't you go to NYU?

HARDBODY BARTENDER. No.

PATRICK. Columbia?

(She's silent.)

...That was a joke.

HARDBODY BARTENDER. Twenty-five dollars.

PATRICK. I have these drink tickets...

HARDBODY BARTENDER. It's after eleven. Those aren't good anymore. Cash bar, twenty-five dollars.

PATRICK. Can you break a fifty?

(She turns away to make change.)

Because if you can't, I'm going to stab you to death and play around with your blood and entrails.

(She turns back; she didn't hear him.)

Keep the change, beautiful.

*(**TIM** finds **PATRICK** again.)*

TIM. Hey!

PATRICK. Price! I figured out where they go.

TIM. What?

PATRICK. The tracks! They go into the Tunnel.

TIM. Oh, Jesus, *fine*, come on –

– let's go to the bathroom. We need to do some Bolivian Marching Powder, like, *now*.

(The lights change. **PATRICK** *and* **TIM** *are in a stall in one of Tunnel's unisex bathrooms, preparing to snort a gram of coke.)*

Jeez, that's not a hell of a lot, is it? What is Ricardo's problem; he said it was a *gram* –

*(***PATRICK*** snorts some.)*

PATRICK. Oh my God...

TIM. What? How is it?

PATRICK. Terrible. It's – it's fucking *Sweet'n Low.*

*(***TIM*** snorts some.)*

TIM. ...I mean, it's definitely not the best, but if we do enough of it, we should be fine –

PATRICK. – I want to get *high* off this, Price, not sprinkle it on my fucking All-Bran!
(Still pissed.) – GOD-DAMN-FUCKING-RICARDO –

[MUSIC NO. 07 "KILLING TIME"]

TIM. *Bateman – chill – and seriously – what is your fucking problem –?*

PATRICK. – *What is my fucking problem??* – *My fucking problem is* – I'm young, I'm skilled, I'm resourceful – I'm an asset society *cannot* afford to lose – And yet, I *hate* my job, *you* hate your job, the world's going *insane,* and we're getting to the point where our bodies have somehow become *attuned* to the insanity, it's started to make sense to us –
THERE'S A FLAW IN THE SYSTEM
THERE'S A CRACK IN THE SKY
I'VE TAKEN THE STEPS
BUT I'M NOT FEELING HIGH

TIM.
THERE'S NOT ENOUGH MONEY
THERE AREN'T ENOUGH GIRLS
PRETTY SURE THOSE ARE SIGNS
IT'S THE END OF THE WORLD

PATRICK.

MAYBE IT'S ME OR IT'S YOU
OR IT'S US
MY HEAD IS ON FIRE
AND THERE IS NO BECAUSE

TIM.

TAKE A DEEP BREATH
YOU'RE JUST SPINNING OUT
I'VE GOT NO IDEA
WHAT YOU'RE TALKIN' ABOUT

YOU DON'T FEEL ALL RIGHT
THAT'S NOT A CRIME
ENJOY THE SPOILS
IGNORE THE GRIME

PATRICK.

SOMEWHERE THE SCENT
OF BURNING LIME

PATRICK & TIM.

WE'RE KILLING TIME,
WE'RE KILLING –

IT'S THE END OF THE WORLD
THE VEIL IS SLIPPING
IT'S THE END OF THE WORLD
I'M NOT JUST TRIPPING

IT'S THE END OF THE WORLD
IT'S RUSHING AT US
IT'S THE END OF THE WORLD
AND NONE OF IT MATTERS

(They emerge from the bathroom. **PATRICK**
and **TIM** *rejoin the rest of the* **CLUBGOERS.***)*

ALL.

YOU LOOK SO GOOD
IT FEELS SO RIGHT
GET A TABLE AND A BOTTLE
AND PUT IT ON ICE
DON'T YOU SEE HEAVEN

IS A STATE OF MIND
WE'RE KILLING TIME
WE'RE KILLING TIME

LOVE WON'T LAST
WON'T LAST FOREVER
WE HAVE TONIGHT
AND WE NEVER SAY NEVER
GET ANOTHER DRINK
DO ANOTHER LINE
WE'RE KILLING TIME
WE'RE KILLING TIME
WE'RE KILLING TIME

(Everything is building...)

PATRICK.

I'M GONNA FIND OUT
I'VE GOTTA KNOW
IT'S AT THE END OF THE TRACKS
THE END OF THE ROAD

'CAUSE I'VE KILLED TIME
TILL IT'S DEAD AND IT'S GONE
NO IN NO OUT
NO RIGHT NO WRONG

SO GOODBYE ALL YOU CUNTS
I'M DONE WITH THESE PLACES
I'M TIRED OF ALL OF YOUR
HIDEOUS FACES

EVERY ONE OF YOU FOOLS
IS A STUPID FUCK
GOOD LUCK
GOOD LUCK
GOOD LUCK
GOOD LUCK!

Oh, screw it! GOODBYE...FUCKHEADS!

*(**PATRICK** starts following the train tracks, disappearing into a literal, as well as metaphoric, tunnel, with **TIM** calling after him:)*

TIM. Bateman! *Wait, Bateman –*

> *(And then* **PATRICK** *goes "down the tunnel," disappearing...)*

> *(...As the crowd and the club melt away...)*

> *(As* **PATRICK** *moves through the streets of New York at night, across the dark stage, a chorus of* **PROSTITUTES** *– including* **CHRISTINE** *and* **SABRINA** *– sing.)*

> **[MUSIC NO. 08 "IN THE AIR TONIGHT"]***

> *[***ENSEMBLE*** sings "In The Air Tonight."]*

> *(***PATRICK***'s wandering has led him to a back alley; he nearly trips over a* **HOMELESS MAN,** *a dirty blanket around his shoulders...)*

PATRICK. Hello.

> *(Holding out his hand.)*

Pat Bateman.

> *(The* **HOMELESS MAN** *ignores* **PATRICK***'s hand.)*

What's your name?

> *(The* **HOMELESS MAN** *mumbles something.)*

...*Al?* Did you say –?

> *(Forget it, doesn't matter –)*

You want some money? Some...food?

> *(The* **HOMELESS MAN** *starts to nod, cry.* **PATRICK** *pulls out a ten-dollar bill.)*

Is this what you need...?

HOMELESS MAN. I'm so hungry...

PATRICK. And it's cold out, too, isn't it...?

HOMELESS MAN. Yes...

PATRICK. Why don't you get a *job*, then? If you're so hungry and cold?

---

*Licensees should refer to their piano/conductor books for the lyrics to Music No. 08 "In The Air Tonight."

HOMELESS MAN. I lost my job...

PATRICK. Why? Insider trading? No, that was a joke.

　(Then:)

　Listen to me. Do you think it's *fair* to take money from people who do have jobs? Who *do* work?

HOMELESS MAN. What can I do?

PATRICK. You know what your problem is, Al? You've got a negative attitude. But guess what? I'll help you.

HOMELESS MAN. You...you're so kind, mister. I can tell.

　*(**PATRICK** kneels down, touches the **HOMELESS MAN**'s face.)*

PATRICK. *Shhhhh...* It's okay...

　(Then:)

　Do you know how *rotten* you smell? The stench, my God, you *reek* of shit –

HOMELESS MAN. Sorry, I'm...

PATRICK. I'm sorry, too, Al. It's just that...*I don't. Have anything. In common. With you.*

　*(And here **PATRICK** pulls a knife out of his jacket pocket and stabs the **HOMELESS MAN**, almost mercifully. Stabs him again and again, and the lights crossfade from this alley to:)*

　*(The Health Club Xclusive. To a **HARDBODY TRAINER** leading her aerobics class.)*

　[MUSIC NO. 09 "HARDBODY"]

MCDERMOTT, VAN PATTEN & LUIS.

　I LIKE 'EM LIKE THAT
　I LIKE A HARDBODY
　I BET THAT AFTER THIS CLASS
　SHE TEACHES DIRTY KARATE

MEN.

　I LIKE 'EM LIKE THAT
　I LIKE A HARDBODY

SHE KEEPS A TIDY RIG
BUT YOU KNOW SHE'S NAUGHTY

HARDBODY TRAINER.

HEY BOY,
STOP TALKING LIKE YOU GOT ME
YOU GOTTA IMPRESS ME
AND I LIKE A HARDBODY

HEY BOY,
YOU THINK THAT YOU CAN HAVE ME?
WELL STOP STARING AT ME
AND WORK YOUR HARDBODY

MEN 1.	**MEN 2.**
WE LIKE 'EM LIKE THAT	(WE LIKE 'EM LIKE THAT)
WE LIKE HARDBODIES	(WE LIKE HARDBODIES)
WE WANT TO TASTE	(WE WANT TO TASTE
THEIR –	THEIR –)
LA DI DA DI	

(The lights shift. We see **PATRICK** *in Courtney's bedroom. They've just finished fucking;* **COURTNEY***'s lighting a cigarette...)*

COURTNEY. What's the rest of your day like?

PATRICK. The gym. Then work. Then a show with Evelyn tonight.

COURTNEY. Which one?

PATRICK. Uhm. What's the one with the little homeless girl on the poster...?

COURTNEY. *(Incredulous at his cluelessness.)* ...Do you mean *Les Miz*?

PATRICK. *(Eureka!)* – YES, exactly, *Les Miz* –

COURTNEY. *(Biting the bullet.)* – Look, Patrick, not to spring this on you, but as much as I *relish* these afternoon trysts...we need to stop.

PATRICK. And why would we do that?

COURTNEY. *(Uh.)* Because I'm Evelyn's best friend – Not to mention, Luis is starting to suspect –

PATRICK. Luis is –

COURTNEY. Don't you call him a homo!

PATRICK. A dork, I was going to say. A twit.

>   *(Beat, moving on.)*

Listen, I'm doing a survey of the women I fuck. Is it my *muscles* that excite you? Or the *heft* of my cock?

COURTNEY. You're not hearing me. We're stopping.

PATRICK. Let me ask you, Courtney. Hypothetically. If something were to happen to Luis – an accident, say, or a violent crime – and he were out of the picture, would you be upset?

COURTNEY. I can't answer that. It's too morbid. I'd be devastated.

>   *(Beat. **PATRICK** is finished getting dressed for the gym.)*

PATRICK. Fine.

>   *(He's done.)*

Awesome.

COURTNEY. I hope – things won't be weird between us now. I hope – we can go back to being friends again.

PATRICK. Courtney?

>   *(And please don't take this the wrong way –)*

You are a babe, but no sex is worth this bullshit.

COURTNEY. Fuck you, you asshole.

>   *(**PATRICK** leaves Courtney's bedroom, and we crossfade to the locker room as **PATRICK** joins the **GUYS** in towels and robes.)*

MCDERMOTT. Our trainer this morning? *Total* hardbody.

VAN PATTEN. Definitely. *Great* tits.

MCDERMOTT. Great ass.

LUIS. I was *not* impressed. Did you see her knees?

MCDERMOTT. Knees? I just want some hot chick who will sit on my face for thirty, forty minutes; is that a crime?

PATRICK. Deep, McDermott, you're a regular Ed Gein.

LUIS. Ed Gein? Is he the maître d' at Canal Bar?

PATRICK. No, Luis, Ed Gein's a serial killer. Said a lot of interesting things about women.

TIM. Jesus Christ, Bateman, not again –

PATRICK. What? Don't piss me off, Price –

VAN PATTEN. He's got a point, though – If you're not talking about your hero, *the Donald*, you're talking about the Son of Sam – or Ted Bundy – or Featherhead –

MCDERMOTT. Featherhead? Who the hell is Featherhead?

TIM. He means *Leatherface*, you idiots –

(To **PATRICK.***)* Part of the original *Texas Chainsaw Massacre*, I believe?

PATRICK. That's right, Price –

(Turning to **VAN PATTEN.***)*

And for the record, Van Patten, *The Art of the Deal* is not just *THE BEST* business advice book ever written, it's also an excellent memoir –

TIM. Who wants to steam? And maybe Bateman can tell us all about the Hillside Strangler, too –

*(***TIM, MCDERMOTT,** *and* **VAN PATTEN** *go, so it's just* **PATRICK** *and* **LUIS** *in the locker room.)*

PATRICK. *(To audience.)* Question: Would I ruin everything by strangling Luis? Or, on the other hand, would the world be a safer, kinder place? The grim truth is, *my* world might be, so...why not?

*(***PATRICK** *reaches* **LUIS,** *who is standing with his back toward the audience at a urinal in the otherwise deserted locker room.* **PATRICK** *goes to strangle* **LUIS** *– he puts his hands on* **LUIS***'s throat – but* **LUIS** *turns to face* **PATRICK,** *completely misinterpreting the moment.)*

LUIS. Jesus, Patrick, why here?

PATRICK. Huh?

LUIS. I've seen you looking at me. I've noticed your –

(He gulps.)

– hard body.

PATRICK. My what?

LUIS. I *want* this; I've *wanted* this. Since that Genesis concert we went to. You were wearing that red striped paisley Armani tie.

PATRICK. *(Pushing* **LUIS** *off.)* Get away from me, Luis –

LUIS. It's okay, I was nervous my first time, too. Nervous – I was terrified. Does Evelyn suspect? I know Courtney doesn't –

PATRICK. I, I have to go – I have to return some videotapes – This *didn't* happen –

> *(***PATRICK*** rushes out, holding his clothes.)*

LUIS. PATRICK – I'll call you –

> *(***PATRICK*** is out of there.)*

> *(As we transition from the locker room to a Broadway theater, various* **ENSEMBLE MEMBERS** *– out for a night of theatre – help us along...)*

[MUSIC NO. 9A "YOU ARE WHAT YOU WEAR – REPRISE 1"]

WOMEN.
WE'RE OFF TO THE THEATER
THE SEATS AREN'T CHEAP

MEN.
I REALLY HOPE
I DON'T FALL ASLEEP

ALL.
WE DON'T NEED TICKETS TO
PHANTOM OF THE OPERA
WE GOT GREAT SEATS
FOR *LES MISÉRABLES*!

WOMEN.
SHALL WE WEAR
THE GOLD BROCADE

> IT TOTALLY SPARKLES
> ON THE BARRICADE!

MEN.

> I WISH I COULD GROW
> FACIAL HAIR
> AND WEAR THE CLOTHES
> JEAN VALJEAN WEARS

> > *(Leading into the last chorus of "One Day More" from* Les Miz, *as a spot finds...***JEAN**, *sitting in a theater box, clutching a* Les Miz *Playbill, tears in her lovely eyes...)*

> > *(Once she's been established, we find* **PATRICK** *and* **EVELYN**, *sitting in an opposite box, on the opposite side of the stage, as the "lights" come up for "intermission.")*

PATRICK. Wow, that was – *wow...*

> *(Standing, woozily.)*

That was – overwhelming – I, I need a drink after that, *fuck* –

EVELYN. Patrick –

PATRICK. – Do you want a drink? A rum and Diet Pepsi?

EVELYN. *Eww,* no, I want you to sit here with me so we can talk. You're giving me ten minutes of your undivided attention –

> > *(***PATRICK** *is looking at* **JEAN** *across the way,* **EVELYN** *notices it.)*

(Annoyed.) – Okay, *who* are you looking at, Patrick, who is so fascinating –?

PATRICK. *(Surprised, as he sits down.)* Jean, my, my secretary, is here –

> > *(***JEAN** *recedes but stays onstage.)*

EVELYN. Where *were* you last night? I called you from the Carlyle, where I checked myself in; you never answered.

PATRICK. I give up: Why were you staying at the Carlyle?

EVELYN. Because the woman who lives in the brownstone next to mine? Was found murdered and *decapitated* yesterday.

PATRICK. Goodness. Well – are *you* all right?

EVELYN. Of course not, I'm *upset*! I went to Elizabeth Arden, to calm myself with a facial, and Mia, my facialist, described me as "tense," which is why: *No tip for Mia –*

> *(Beat.)*

But stop dodging: Where *were* you last night?

PATRICK. I was packing your neighbor's head in ice in my freezer –

EVELYN. I mean it: I wanted to come over and discuss something *extremely* important and *you* weren't home –

PATRICK. – I was renting some videotapes –

> *(Then, careful:)*

Discuss what, exactly?

EVELYN. The future. How we should just do it.

PATRICK. Do what?

EVELYN. Get married. Have a wedding. We'll announce at my Christmas party. Your mom will be there –

PATRICK. Evelyn, darling, are you having a stroke?

[MUSIC NO. 10 "IF WE GET MARRIED"]

EVELYN. *(Off and running.)* I'd want a sixteen-foot tiered Ben and Jerry's ice cream cake…a gown by Ralph, thousands of roses, and, and – Annie Leibovitz! And someone to videotape it! To make it real. Oh, Patrick –

IF WE GET MARRIED
WE'LL START A NEW LIFE

PATRICK.

I'M HAVING A NIGHTMARE
WHERE YOU ARE MY WIFE

EVELYN.

I'D LIKE A HUGE DIAMOND
WON'T SETTLE FOR LESS

PATRICK.

> HOW MANY CARATS?
> OR SHOULD I JUST GUESS?
> IF YOU ONLY KNEW...

JEAN.

> IF I ONLY KNEW...

EVELYN.

> IF WE GET MARRIED...

JEAN.

> WOULD I BE HAPPY...?

PATRICK.

> IF YOU ONLY KNEW...

JEAN.

> IF HE GOT MARRIED
> HE MIGHT RELAX

EVELYN.

> I'D SERVE HIM DINNER

PATRICK.

> I'D SWING AN AXE

JEAN.

> IT'S THAT LOOK IN HIS EYE
> THAT I DON'T UNDERSTAND

EVELYN.

> I'LL BURST INTO TEARS
> WHEN HE TAKES MY HAND...

JEAN.

> WHEN HE HOLDS HER HAND...

PATRICK.

> WHEN I CUT OFF HER HAND...
> IF YOU ONLY KNEW...

JEAN.

> IF I ONLY KNEW...

EVELYN.

> IF WE GET MARRIED...

JEAN.

> WOULD I BE HAPPY...

PATRICK.

    IF YOU ONLY KNEW...

JEAN.

    IF I ONLY KNEW...

EVELYN.

    IF WE GET MARRIED...

PATRICK.

    IF YOU ONLY KNEW...

    (Then:)

Jeez, Evelyn, I don't know...

EVELYN. What are you going to do? Wait three years until you're *thirty*?

PATRICK. Did I tell you I'm wearing sixty-dollar boxer shorts?

EVELYN. *Aaarrggh*, you're impossible! A – a *real* party pooper –

    (She stands to go.)

And if I call you tonight from the Carlyle – which I *won't*, since I'm *livid* with you – you had *better* answer!

[MUSIC NO. 10A "IN THE AIR TONIGHT – REPRISE"]*

    *(**EVELYN** exits.)*

PATRICK. *(To audience.)* Though it would make my life so much easier in so many ways if Evelyn just – *stopped breathing*, I...don't go after her. And there's no reason for this choice – *my* choice. It's simply how the world – *my* world – moves tonight...

    *(**PATRICK** moves from the theater, gets into a limo, instructs his **DRIVER**.)*

The Meatpacking District.

    *(They "pull up" next to a **PROSTITUTE**. **PATRICK** lowers his window.)*

---

*Licensees should refer to their piano/conductor books for the lyrics to Music No. 10a "In The Air Tonight – Reprise."

PATRICK. Hi, there. Do you take American Express?

> (*She stares at him blankly.*)

I'm kidding. What's your name?

CHRISTINE. Christine.

PATRICK. Christine, I'm...*Paul*, Paul Owen. Would you like to see my apartment?

CHRISTINE. I'm not supposed to...

PATRICK. Come on, get in. I have another friend coming over, Christine, I think you'll like her... Climb in.

> (**CHRISTINE** *"gets into" the limo as we hear:*)
>
> [**PROSTITUTES** *sing* "In The Air Tonight – Reprise."]
>
> (*The action shifts to Patrick's apartment, where another prostitute,* **SABRINA***, is sipping a Chardonnay, looking at the David Onica painting.**)

PATRICK. Sabrina, this is Christine. Christine, Sabrina. Sabrina, did you clean yourself?

SABRINA. Yes...

> (**PATRICK** *starts pouring* **CHRISTINE** *a Chardonnay.*)

PATRICK. Good. I saw you admiring that Onica, do you like it?

SABRINA. What? Sorry?

PATRICK. The painting. It's by an artist named David Onica. Quite expensive. Fifty thousand.

> (*He hands* **CHRISTINE** *a glass of wine.*)

SABRINA. Fifty thousand seems like...a lot.

PATRICK. I don't know, I think his work has a kind of... wonderfully proportioned, purposefully mock-superficial quality...

---

*Licensees do not have rights to prints by either Man Ray or David Onica and should create original images in the style of these artists.

CHRISTINE. You have a nice place here, Paul. How much did you pay for it?

PATRICK. Actually, that's none of your business, but I can assure you, it certainly wasn't cheap.

(Charming/annoyed.) And *that* is a very fine Chardonnay you're not drinking, Christine.

> (**CHRISTINE** *drinks.*)

Now would either of you ladies like to know what I do for a living?

CHRISTINE. Not really.

SABRINA. Are you a model?

PATRICK. No. Flattering, but no. I work on Wall Street, at Pierce and Pierce. Have you heard of it?

SABRINA. Sure. It's a shoe store, right?

PATRICK. It's an investment bank.

CHRISTINE. What do you do there?

PATRICK. I'm into, oh, murders and executions, mostly. It depends.

SABRINA. Do you like it?

PATRICK. Uhm, it depends. Why do you ask?

SABRINA. 'Cause most guys I know who work in mergers and acquisitions don't really like it.

PATRICK. Yes, but I handle a very important account, the *Fisher* account, and anyway that's not what I said. I *said* –

> *(Beat.)*

Oh, forget it. Let's just get started –

> *(And they do. They all strip, the* **WOMEN** *start dancing.* **PATRICK** *watches, then joins in, singing himself into godhood –)*

[MUSIC NO. 11 "NOT A COMMON MAN"]

LOOK AT HISTORY
OPEN THE BOOKS
THERE ARE STATUES WITH GREAT LOOKS

THERE ARE GODS, THERE ARE KINGS
I'M PRETTY SURE I'M THE SAME THING

BEYOND BOUNDARIES
BEYOND RULES
I'VE BEEN TAUGHT IN THE BEST SCHOOLS
THERE IS LITTLE I WON'T DO
I'M NOT LIKE YOU

PATRICK & ENSEMBLE.

I AM NEEDING
SO MUCH MORE
EVERY PLEASURE IS A BORE
I AM SOMETHING OTHER THAN
A COMMON MAN, I'M NOT A COMMON MAN

> (**PATRICK** *is looking at himself fucking the*
> **WOMEN**...*)*

PATRICK.

YOU SHOULD STAY CALM, REMAIN COMPLIANT
I'M PROBABLY NOT YOUR AVERAGE CLIENT
REMEMBER GIRLS – THIS IS MANHATTAN

STAY UP LATE – YOU KNOW, THINGS HAPPEN

LOOK AT THE MOON, SEE IT WAX
IT WILL HURT LESS IF YOU RELAX
ARE YOU EXCITED OR AFRAID?
EITHER WAY, YOU WILL BE PAID

PATRICK & ENSEMBLE.

I AM NEEDING
SO MUCH MORE
EVERY PLEASURE IS A BORE
I AM SOMETHING OTHER THAN
A COMMON MAN, I'M NOT A COMMON MAN

ARE YOU LOSING TOO MUCH BLOOD?
LET IT FLOW, LET IT FLOOD
JUST KEEP BREATHING IF YOU CAN
YOU WILL SEE, I'M NOT A COMMON MAN

THERE IS NO REASON, NO REMORSE
JUST THE NEED TO STAY THE COURSE
I THOUGHT YOU'D HELP ME TO UNDERSTAND

THAT I'M NOT, I'M NOT A COMMON MAN

I AM NOT HERE
I AM NOT THERE
I AM NOBODY
I AM NOWHERE

I AM NOT HERE
I AM NOT THERE
I AM NOBODY
I AM NOWHERE

Tomorrow, Sabrina will have a limp. Christine will have a black eye and lacerations on her back from a coathanger. They will have left my apartment bleeding, but compensated.

> *(When the song ends, **PATRICK** crosses from his apartment to his office, starts getting dressed in a tuxedo. **JEAN**, holding a Christmas present, softly singing "Silent Night," crosses toward him, catches him in the middle of putting his shirt on.)*

JEAN.
SILENT NIGHT, HOLY NIGHT
ALL IS CALM

> *(Seeing him shirtless.)*

– Oh, Patrick, I'm so sorry, I thought you were still at lunch –

> *(Actually, **PATRICK** doesn't mind it, at all. Dresses even slower, in fact...)*

PATRICK. It's okay, Jean, come on in.

JEAN. Patrick, I, uh. Sent out all 300 of your Christmas cards. They're beautiful.

PATRICK. Mark Kostabi designed them. Limited edition, only available this year.

JEAN. Very fancy.

> *(Awkward beat.)*

Well, if there's nothing else...

PATRICK. *(Awkward, but trying.)* What – what are you doing for Christmas, Jean? Are you – going home?

JEAN. Staying in New York. My sister's coming to visit, she got us tickets to *Les Miz* – I'm pretending I haven't seen it.

PATRICK. *(Re: EVELYN.)* Some people think it doesn't live up to the hype, but –

    (A test?)

– did you like it?

JEAN. I loved it.

PATRICK. *(Giddy, earnest.)* – ME TOO! It was so beautiful and emotional – especially Fantine's tour-de-force solo, "I Dreamed a Dream," which (it's safe to say) could be one of the most important ballads of the twentieth century –

JEAN. I know, I – I cried. It's such an uplifting, human story.

PATRICK. Isn't it? And the Innkeeper and his wife, they were *hilarious*. I can't get that song, "Master of the House," out of my head – so witty –

JEAN. *(She smiles.)* Big plans for Christmas?

PATRICK. Hanging with my family, escorting my mother to Evelyn's Christmas party…

JEAN. I thought you two were in a lovers' spat or something.

PATRICK. We were, but then…this kind of existential chasm opened up in front of me while I was shopping at Bloomingdale's, and… I don't know… 'Tis the season.

JEAN. *We-ell…*

    (Holding out the gift.)

This is for you. Merry Christmas, Patrick.

PATRICK. Merry Christmas, Jean.

[MUSIC NO. 12 "MISTLETOE ALERT"]

(JEAN exits, and PATRICK – and we – go to… Evelyn's Christmas party, in full swing. EVELYN wears a Santa hat and carries a sprig

of mistletoe. **COURTNEY** *and* **MRS. BATEMAN** *are there. As* **PATRICK** *joins them in the tableau:)*

(To audience.) As with many people, the holidays are a difficult time for me. So, I bolster myself with daily viewings of *Silent Night, Deadly Night,* a *superb* movie about an axe-wielding Santa. I lace my hot apple cider with copious amounts of drugs and alcohol to dull the screaming. I prepare my apartment for a Christmas Eve bacchanal/bloodbath. Whose, I don't know yet...

(Then:)

That's my Christmas present to myself.

EVELYN & PARTY GUESTS.

MISTLETOE!
MISTLETOE ALERT!

M-I-S-T-L-E-TOE

MISTLETOE!
MISTLETOE ALERT...

EVELYN.

I WANT A PARTY
TO REMEMBER
THE BEST OF THIS
NEW YORK DECEMBER

A FABULOUS
AND PERFECT FÊTE
A PARTY NO ONE
WILL FORGET

EVELYN & PARTY GUESTS.

MISTLETOE!
MISTLETOE ALERT!

M-I-S-T-L-E-TOE

MISTLETOE!
MISTLETOE ALERT...

PATRICK.	**ALL OTHERS.**
NOW THAT'S ENOUGH OF TRADITION	AH

AND HOLIDAY CHEER	AH
IT'S TIME FOR THE TERROR	AH
AND THE SWEET SMELL OF FEAR	AH
SO GIRD YOUR LOINS	AH, AH
AND CLUTCH YOUR PEARLS	AH, AH
I'M READY TO BUTCHER	AH, AH
SOME BOYS AND SOME GIRLS	AH, AH
SOME FUCKING LEAVES	MISTLETOE
ABOVE THE DOOR	MISTLETOE
AND A BLOODY CARCASS	MISTLETOE
SPLAYED ON THE FLOOR	HO HO HO HO

(The party around **PATRICK** *distorts.* **EVELYN** *notices* **PATRICK***'s demeanor...)*

EVELYN. Oh, stop *scowling*, Patrick, you're such a Grinch. Isn't he, Mrs. Bateman? Isn't Patrick *such* a Grinch?

MRS. BATEMAN. Where's the *bar*, Evelyn?

EVELYN. Oh – uh – over there, being tended by Frosty the Snowman –

    (MCDERMOTT *and* **VAN PATTEN,** *both of them wearing antlers, approach* **PATRICK***...)*

MCDERMOTT. – *BATEMAN*, hey, man, are you *on* something?

VAN PATTEN. – And, if so, can we score some *off* you?

PATRICK. – Oh, so many things. I *may*, in fact, be having an anxiety attack –

VAN PATTEN. Jesus, low-point of the evening much?

MCDERMOTT. Yeah, if you don't want to share, just say so –

    (They go.)

COURTNEY. *(Grabbing* **LUIS**.*)* – Evelyn, have I told you? What Luis got me for Christmas? You know the artist Jean-Michel Basquiat, of course?

EVELYN. *(Gasps.)* – *Of course* – Luis, you sneak – I, personally, would *love* to have an original *anything*, under my tree, Christmas morning –

PATRICK. Courtney's head in a hat box? A necklace made of Luis's fingers?

EVELYN. As long as there's a ring on one of those fingers – – Luis, come with me, I need your help at the buffet –

> *(****EVELYN*** and **LUIS** go, leaving **COURTNEY** *alone with* **PATRICK**. *She's drunk, pleased with herself...)*

COURTNEY. I hope you like Evelyn's Christmas gift – I helped her pick it out –

PATRICK. *(Excited, like a kid.)* Is it a Black and Decker 20-Volt MAX Lithium Cordless chainsaw?? From my wish list??

COURTNEY. It's a *raincoat*, from *Burberry* –

> *(As* **COURTNEY** *goes –)*
>
> *(–* **LUIS** *arrives.)*

LUIS. I saw you talking to Courtney, Patrick. You didn't tell her about us, did you?

PATRICK. "Us"? Luis, no, there is no "us."

LUIS. Patrick, what are we doing here?

PATRICK. Me? Personally? I'm *tripping* – *Badly* – As for you? I think you're trying to give me *head*!

LUIS. Not here – *Never* here –

> *(****PAUL*** *revolves on –)*

PAUL. – Marcus!

> *(****LUIS*** goes, and **PATRICK** *smiles.)*

PATRICK. ...*PAUL!*

(Indeed, it is **PAUL** *at Evelyn's Christmas party, which fades away as* **PATRICK** *approaches him...)*

PAUL. Jesus Christ, Merry X-mas!

PATRICK. Paul –

(He pulls himself together.)

Merry X-mas, Paul.

PAUL. How the hell have you been, Halberstam? Workaholic, I suppose.

PATRICK. You...you know me. And you? Workaholic?

PAUL. Just closed down shop for the holidays. One last meeting at the Knickerbocker. Now, here I am! At Evelyn Williams's Christmas party!

PATRICK. Evelyn Williams... Who is still dating –

PAUL. That douchebag Patrick Bateman? So I hear.

PATRICK. What a – such a douche.

PAUL. Is Cecilia here tonight?

PATRICK. She...she has the flu.

PAUL. Say, Marcus, it's pretty dead here – you wanna cut out together?

PATRICK. *(Does he?)* The Christmas midgets are about to sing "O Tannenbaum" –

PAUL. You still hankering for Dorsia? *Amazing* sea urchin there this time of year –

PATRICK. – Great, yeah, let's do that...

(This is it!)

...but let's swing by my place first.

*(**PATRICK** and **PAUL** cross to Patrick's apartment, which slides on. **PATRICK** maneuvers **PAUL** to sit down on a chair in the middle of the living room. He gets **PAUL**, who is drunk, a drink, then goes to his jukebox, starts a song playing. **PATRICK** sings along, dancing as well.)*

[MUSIC NO. 13 "HIP TO BE SQUARE"]*

[PATRICK and PAUL sing mm. 8-51 of "Hip To Be Square."]

(Beat, excited:)

PATRICK. So – you like Huey Lewis and the News?

PAUL. Maybe. They did...*Back to the Future*, right?

PATRICK. In a sense. They recorded two songs for the movie, "The Power of Love" and "Back in Time," which I consider...delightful footnotes to what is shaping up to be a legendary career. Their masterpiece, though, in *my* opinion, is "Hip to be Square." Have you ever *listened* to it, Paul? I mean, the lyrics?

PAUL. Uh...

PATRICK. It's okay. With Chris Hayes blasting guitar and the terrific keyboard playing, who cares about lyrics, right? The song's so damn catchy, most people don't realize it's a rollicking ode to conformity and the importance of trends. Not to mention a personal statement about the band, itself.

PAUL. *(Feeling it.)* God, I'm drunker than I thought...

PATRICK. That's the date-rape drug I put in your drink.

PAUL. Oh, is that why I'm feeling...mellow?

PATRICK. Paul. About the Fisher account. Tell me. How did you come to acquire it?

PAUL. One of those things. I guess they thought I would be the best person to...take it to the next level.

PATRICK. Right. Of course. And...Dorsia? How is it that you're always able to score reservations at Dorsia? Silly thing, but I've always wondered.

PAUL. I'm friends with the maître d'.

PATRICK. Interesting...

[PATRICK and PAUL sing mm. 55-79 of "Hip To Be Square."]

---

*Licensees should refer to their piano/conductor books for the lyrics to Music No. 13 "Hip To Be Square."

(Beat.)

PATRICK. I was taking a piss in the men's room at the Yale Club, Paul, and I was staring into this thin...web-like crack above the urinal's handle, and it started me thinking: "If I were to, say, somehow miniaturize and disappear into that crack...the odds are good no one would notice I was gone. *No one...would...care.*" "In fact," I thought, *"If* they noticed my absence, they might even feel an odd, indefinable sense of relief." That's when I realized *this* truth, Paul. *(Look at me.)*

(**PAUL** *does.*)

The world *is* better off with some people gone... Our lives are *not* all interconnected... Some people do *not* need to be here...

PAUL. Marcus...is that a raincoat you're wearing?

PATRICK. Yes, it is, but it's all right, Evelyn's giving me a new one for Christmas. From Burberry.

PAUL. Evelyn...Williams? Why would Evelyn Williams be giving *you* a raincoat for Christmas?

(Looking down.)

And, uh, why are there copies of the Style section all over the floor? Do you have a dog? A chow or something?

PATRICK. No, I put them down in case I killed Luis or Courtney or Evelyn tonight, but that was before...

PAUL. Before...?

PATRICK. I'm utterly insane, Paul! I like to dissect girls!

PAUL. It's fine, I used to hate Iggy Pop, too, but now that he's more commercial, I like him.

(**PATRICK** *reveals an "oh shit" silver axe he had stashed around a corner.* **PAUL** *is out of it, not looking at* **PATRICK**...)

PATRICK. We're both twenty-seven years old, did you know that?

(Beat.)

Paul?

> [**PATRICK** *and* **PAUL** *sing mm. 81-82 of "Hip To Be Square."*]

PATRICK. *Fucking! Stupid! Bastard!*

> [**PATRICK** *and* **PAUL** *sing m. 84 of "Hip To Be Square."*]

> (**PAUL** *turns to look at* **PATRICK** – *as* **PATRICK** *brings the axe down on* **PAUL***'s face. Over and over again.*)

> (*On the first strike of the axe, "Hip to be Square" blasts to an almost head-splitting intensity.*)

> (*The violence is bloody, shocking, exhausting.* **PATRICK** *finishes killing* **PAUL***, however long that takes, but way beyond comfortable...*)

ACT TWO

[MUSIC NO. 14 "CLEAN"]

*(A tight spot finds **PATRICK**, surrounded by darkness.)*

PATRICK. *(To audience.)* It takes Paul Owen five minutes to die. Another thirty to stop bleeding. I know, because I time it, on my classic Rolex Datejust.

(Then:)

Afterwards, still wearing the bloody raincoat, I take a cab to Paul's apartment on the Upper East Side; I let myself in with his keys –

*(The lights bump up, revealing Paul's apartment, which looks suspiciously like... Patrick's apartment. Very bright, very white. **PATRICK** looks around...)*

A plan is taking shape in the folds of my brain, but where should I "send" Paul on a business trip? Amsterdam? Rome? Phoenix?

*(Like a ghost, or a voice inside Patrick's head, we discover **PAUL** standing on the fringes of the stage, a bloody mess, looking at **PATRICK**.)*

PAUL.	PATRICK.
London –	*(Sudden inspiration.)*
	London! I'll send the bastard to England!
My answering machine –	His answering machine –
Our voices are similar enough –	

PAUL. "Hi, this is Paul Owen" –

PATRICK. *(Recording the message.)* "Hi, this is Paul Owen. I'm sorry I'm not here to receive your call, but I'm in *London* for the next two weeks, taking the Fisher account to the next level. If this is something business-related, please call my office."

I pack one of his Ralph Lauren suitcases with his passport and an assortment of toiletries. Then I go back to my place –

> *(The lights shift; we're back in Patrick's apartment, with two **PAULS** now. The dead body, which has just come up on the trap, and the "**GHOST PAUL**" in **PATRICK**'s mind, who continues observing.)*

(To audience.) – where Paul's dead body is already in rigor mortis. I zip him up in a Canalino goose-down sleeping bag I got at Conran's (on sale) –

> *(**PATRICK** "turns back," now holding Paul's wrapped-up corpse in his arms, Creature from the Black Lagoon–style; the lights shift; **PATRICK** is now in front of his building.)*

DOORMAN. Would you like a hand with that, Mr. Bateman?

PATRICK. Thank you, Lloyd. I've ordered a car.

> *(He hands the corpse to the **DOORMAN**.)*

DOORMAN. I believe it's idling by the delivery entrance, sir. I'll get this loaded, then have it circle around to the front.

PATRICK. Thank you, Lloyd. Oh, and Lloyd? My secretary sent you an envelope, didn't she? With a little something for Christmas?

DOORMAN. Yes, sir. The card was beautiful – Mark Kostabi, wasn't it? Thank you, sir.

> *(The **DOORMAN** exits, taking the body with him.)*

PATRICK. This is what happens next: I take the thing that was once Paul Owen to an apartment I own, anonymously, in an abandoned building in Hell's Kitchen. I place it in an oversized porcelain tub and pour a bag of lime over the corpse. I watch as it dissolves into anonymity –

(We hear this.)

Then I take the car (which I had wait for me) back home. I am relieved no one has seen me, but in the elevator going up –

(Ding! The lights change; we're on the elevator with **PATRICK** *and a man wearing sunglasses. He looks a lot like* **TOM CRUISE**.*)*

Merry Christmas.

(Silence from the man.)

It's great, isn't it? This building. Your penthouse must be –

TOM CRUISE. *(Interrupting.)* I like it.

PATRICK. I thought...you were very good in *Top Gun*. I thought it was quite a good movie. And *Bartender*, too. I really thought that one was exceptionally good.

TOM CRUISE. *Cocktail.*

PATRICK. Pardon?

TOM CRUISE. The film was called *Cocktail*, not *Bartender*.

PATRICK. *Cocktail*, that's right. Anyway, I'm a big fan. It's good to meet you, finally, after living in the same building for so many years.

TOM CRUISE. Right.

PATRICK. I – have those same aviators. A lot of people say we look alike.

*(***TOM CRUISE** *slowly turns to* **PATRICK**... *Stares at him for a long while.)*

TOM CRUISE. I don't see it.

(Ding! **TOM CRUISE** *goes, leaving* **PATRICK** *alone on stage, talking to the audience.)*

[MUSIC NO. 15 "KILLING SPREE"]

PATRICK. December slides into January, which mutates into February, which creeps towards March. There is a theory that obliterating Paul *might* have...satisfied something, but...no, I've continued to have intense dreams about vivisection. My nightly bloodlust overflows into my waking life...

> *(Sudden music, sudden lights.* **PATRICK** *is in a club, singing to/dancing with a* **HARDBODY** *he's stalking. The* **GUYS** – **MCDERMOTT, VAN PATTEN,** *et al. – are in the background, singing back-up.)*

HEY PRETTY GIRL
DO YOU WANNA DANCE?
DO YOU WANNA GET LUCKY?
WELL THIS IS YOUR CHANCE

THE DRINKS ARE ON ME
CAN I BE FRANK?
I'M DOING QUITE WELL
AT MY INVESTMENT BANK

WHAT DO YOU DO?
WHAT DO YOU DO FOR A LIVING?
NO, DON'T ANSWER THAT
I DON'T CARE, I'M JUST KIDDING
YOU CAN IGNORE
MY FRIENDS AT THE BAR
THEY'RE TRYING TO SCORE
BUT THEY NEVER GET FAR

> *(**PATRICK** stabs the **HARDBODY** to death.)*

> *(A beep. Spot on **EVELYN**, on the phone with **PATRICK**.)*

EVELYN. Pat-trick, I thought we were having dinner? I thought we had reservations at Raw Space?

PATRICK. Sorry, Evelyn, I had to rent some videotapes –

> *(Beat.)*

I mean, I had to *return* some videotapes –

> *(Beat.)*

I mean, I had to kill this fag and his fag-dog on Sixty-Seventh Street –

EVELYN. Oh, Mr. Bateman, *j'adore* your sense of humor...

> *(Lights change.* **PATRICK,** *in another club, dancing with another, even hotter* **HARDBODY.***)*

PATRICK.
> THAT WAS SOME GIRL
> I FORGET HER NAME
> SHE THINKS WE'RE IN LOVE
> DOES SHE THINK I'M INSANE?
>
> SHE'S NOT IMPORTANT
> JUST KIND OF ANNOYING
> THAT'S A FINE CHARDONNAY
> YOU'RE NOT ENJOYING
>
> OH NEVER MIND
> LET'S QUIT THIS DIVE
> MY WHITE M3
> IS PARKED OUTSIDE
>
> I'LL CALL MY DEALER
> HIS PRODUCT IS CLEAN
> I DON'T WANT TO DRIVE
> LET'S GET A LIMOUSINE

> *(***PATRICK** *kills the* **HARDBODY.***)*

> *(Spot on* **LUIS,** *on the phone with* **PATRICK.***)*

LUIS. Hey, Patrick, am I catching you at a bad time?

PATRICK. – Luis – it is *always* a bad time for me –

LUIS. Well, sort of spur of the moment, but I booked us a room at the St. Regis – under the name Professor Plum –

PATRICK. *Luis – Leave me the fuck alone or I* will *decapitate you –*

LUIS. I hear the words you're saying, but you need to hear *my* words: I love you very, very much –

> *(Over the rest of the song, a montage of* **PATRICK** *killing multiple people.)*

PATRICK.
> OH THIS IS RICH
> I SHOULDN'T SAY

BUT THIS GUY AT WORK
IS TOTALLY GAY

BUT DON'T MIND THAT
WE SHOULD "FOLLOW OUR BLISS"
I KNOW A GREAT SPOT
IT'S CALLED THE ABYSS

OR EVEN BETTER
LET'S GO BACK TO MY PLACE
WE'LL HAVE AN AFTER-PARTY
I CAN EAT YOUR FACE

DON'T BE NERVOUS
INVITE YOUR FRIENDS
THE NIGHT IS YOUNG
BUT IT ALL DEPENDS...

> *(The song ends with* **PATRICK** *arriving at Pierce and Pierce, all jacked, on a blood-high, interrupted by:)*

JEAN. Patrick –

PATRICK. – *Jean!* How are you, Jean? That is a *fantastic* skirt you're wearing! You look *spectacular* –

JEAN. – Your mother's here.

PATRICK. *What?* My *mom* is?

JEAN. You scheduled lunch with her?

PATRICK. Cancel it. Say no. Say I'm –

JEAN. Patrick, she's here, and she's your mother.

PATRICK. *(Losing it.)* I can't face her, Jean. Two hours alone with with –

JEAN. *(Volunteering.)* – I'll go with you.

PATRICK. You?

JEAN. *(Admitting.)* If you want. I mean...*I'd* like to get to know Patrick Bateman's mother.

PATRICK. *(Salvation!)* Jean, that is a *brilliant* idea! Do we need reservations?

> *(Patrick's* **MOTHER** *enters, joins* **PATRICK** *and* **JEAN.***)*

MRS. BATEMAN. I went ahead and made us some, darling. Tavern on the Green.

PATRICK. *(To audience.)* After lunch, we sit in the park...

MRS. BATEMAN. *(To* **JEAN.***)* ...We'd take the train into the city, Patty and I. He loved visiting the Egyptian mummies at the Met.

JEAN. – Me, too.

> *(Then, shyly:)*

I mean, I only went to the Met once, when I was twelve, with my sister, but we spent all day there. Every room was like this...universe...

PATRICK. *(To audience, emotional.)* For one brief moment, I imagine myself with Jean... We're holding hands, running ahead of my mother, across the Great Lawn; we buy balloons, we let them go, we watch them float into the sky...

MRS. BATEMAN. You know, darling, if you married *this* one, maybe you'd be less unhappy.

PATRICK. I'm not unhappy, Mom.

> *(Then:)*

Anyway, Jean would *never* marry someone like me, would you, Jean?

JEAN. I...

> *(Changing subjects.)*

...Uhm, what other secrets can you tell me about Patrick from when he was growing up?

MRS. BATEMAN.	**PATRICK.**
He –	Don't answer that, Mom –

> *(Beat, then:)*

MRS. BATEMAN. ...He was perfect, my perfect little angel.

[MUSIC NO. 16 "NICE THOUGHT"]

HE WAS A BEAUTIFUL CHILD
HE MADE ME LAUGH, HE MADE ME SMILE
A GOLDEN PATH WAS PAVED

STILL, HE WAS SO WELL BEHAVED

AND IT'S A FUNNY THING
HE LOVED TO DANCE
HE LOVED TO SING
SUCH BEAUTIFUL BLOND CURLS
I KNEW ONE DAY HE'D RULE THE WORLD

JEAN.

IT'S A NICE THOUGHT
PATRICK AS A LITTLE CHILD
PLAYING AT THE SEASIDE
HIS SPIRIT FREE, HIS LAUGHTER WILD

IT'S A NICE THOUGHT
TO THINK THAT UNDERNEATH
HE'S BARING A SWEET SOUL
NOT JUST PERFECT TEETH

MRS. BATEMAN.	**EVELYN.**
I SHOULDN'T SAY IT OUT LOUD	PATRICK...
BUT YOU KNOW HE MAKES HIS MOTHER PROUD	BATEMAN...
	(Add **COURTNEY.***)*
I HOPE HE'LL SETTLE DOWN	PATRICK...
HE'D BE SO GREAT WITH KIDS AROUND	BATEMAN...
	(Add **VANDEN, VICTORIA, CHRISTINE,** *and* **SABRINA.***)*
AND YOU SEEM SWEET NOT LIKE THE OTHER GIRLS I MEET	PATRICK...
YOU TWO WOULD LOOK SO NICE TOGETHER	BATEMAN...
	(Add **WOMEN.***)*
IF YOU TOOK THE TIME AND YOU KNEW HIM BETTER	PATRICK...

JEAN.	MRS. BATEMAN.	ENSEMBLE.
TELL ME	I'LL TELL YOU	MMM
ABOUT HIM	ABOUT HIM	
I WANT TO	UNDERSTAND	AH
UNDERSTAND	HIM	
HIM		
MAYBE	MAYBE	MAY
IT'S CRAZY	IT'S CRAZY	BE
IF I SAVE HIM	SAVE HIM	SAVE
WILL IT SAVE		
ME?		
SAVE HIM	SAVE HIM, IT'S A	HIM

MRS. BATEMAN & JEAN.
  NICE THOUGHT

JEAN.	WOMEN.
BUT IT'S JUST A	NICE THOUGHT
DAYDREAM	
GETTING TO KNOW HIM	KNOW HIM
IS HARDER THAN IT MAY	
SEEM	

MRS. BATEMAN & JEAN.

IT'S A NICE THOUGHT	NICE

JEAN.

BUT STILL A LITTLE SCARY	THOUGHT
SOMETHING INSIDE ME	SCARY
KNOWS I SHOULD BE	
WARY	

MRS. BATEMAN & JEAN.   **WOMEN.**

IT'S A NICE THOUGHT	NICE THOUGHT
AH	AH
PATRICK... BATEMAN...	PATRICK... BATEMAN...

PATRICK. *(To audience, spoken over the above music.)* Later, sitting at my desk, I try to remember something, *anything*, from my childhood, but...there...is...nothing.

> (**JEAN** and **MRS. BATEMAN** *continue on their way, leaving* **PATRICK** *alone...*)

MRS. BATEMAN. *(Voice-over, from the darkness.)* Patrick?

PATRICK. *(A little boy.)* Mom?

JEAN. *(Voice-over.)* No, Patrick, it's me, Jean –

> *(The lights change. **JEAN** appears, a bit shaken.*
> *We're at Pierce and Pierce, in Patrick's office.*
> *He looks hungover, sitting behind his desk.)*

There's a Detective...Donald Kimball here to see you. On some kind of official business.

PATRICK. Tell him – tell him I'm at lunch.

JEAN. I think he knows you're here, and – it's almost five...

PATRICK. *(Beat.)* ...Send him in, I guess.

> *(**JEAN** goes, **DETECTIVE KIMBALL** comes in.)*

DETECTIVE KIMBALL. Sorry to barge in, I should've made an appointment. I'm Donald Kimball.

PATRICK. Patrick Bateman. Pat Bateman.

> *(They shake hands.)*

What's the topic of discussion, Detective?

DETECTIVE KIMBALL. I'm investigating the disappearance of Paul Owen.

PATRICK. I see. Well, I haven't heard anything about that. I mean, it hasn't been on Page Six, at least...

DETECTIVE KIMBALL. *(Smiles.)* These are just preliminary questions for my files. What's your address, Mr. Bateman?

PATRICK. Fifty-five, West Eighty-First Street. The American Gardens Building.

DETECTIVE KIMBALL. Nice. Very nice.

PATRICK. Thanks.

DETECTIVE KIMBALL. Doesn't Tom Cruise live there?

PATRICK. He does. The penthouse. In fact, I was *just* talking to Tom...well, I guess it was a few months ago now. Christmas Eve, in fact. God. Jesus. Time dies.

> *(Beat.)*

Flies. Time...flies.

DETECTIVE KIMBALL. Christmas Eve is the night Paul Owen went missing.

PATRICK. *(Beat, WTF is Patrick doing?)* Is it? I was at my girlfriend's Christmas party that evening, then bumped into Tom...later in the night.

DETECTIVE KIMBALL. Your girlfriend is – Evelyn Williams?

PATRICK. Yes, which she would happily corroborate if you asked her.

DETECTIVE KIMBALL. That won't be necessary, Mr. Bateman. What can you tell me about Paul Owen?

PATRICK. Who? Paul? Well, you know, the thing about Paul is...he was a part of that whole...Yale thing.

DETECTIVE KIMBALL. The Yale thing being...?

PATRICK. We-ell, I think, for one, Paul is *probably* a closeted homosexual who does a *lot* of cocaine... *That* Yale thing.

DETECTIVE KIMBALL. But what kind of man was he?

PATRICK. I hope I'm not being cross-examined here...

DETECTIVE KIMBALL. Do you feel that way?

PATRICK. Paul Owen led an orderly life, Detective. As far as I know, he ate a balanced diet.

DETECTIVE KIMBALL. There's a message on Paul's answering machine saying he went to London –

PATRICK. The Fisher account, sure, that makes (sense) –

DETECTIVE KIMBALL. *(Overriding.)* – But his girlfriend doesn't think so.

PATRICK. Have you consulted a psychic?

DETECTIVE KIMBALL. No. But that's a good idea.

PATRICK. Do you suspect foul play?

DETECTIVE KIMBALL. Can't say. It's so strange, though. One day, someone's walking around, going to work, alive, and then...

PATRICK. The Earth...

DETECTIVE KIMBALL. The what?

PATRICK. The Earth just...opens up and swallows people, I guess. People just disappear. Eerie.

DETECTIVE KIMBALL. Listen, I've taken up enough of your time –

PATRICK. Well, I *do* have an early lunch with Cliff Huxtable at the Four Seasons –

DETECTIVE KIMBALL. Here's my card, Mr. Bateman. If anything occurs to you, any information at all –

PATRICK. *(Taking Kimball's card.)* Nice.

DETECTIVE KIMBALL. Nothing special.

PATRICK. Say, Detective. Could there be a connection between Paul's disappearance and all these murders I keep reading about?

DETECTIVE KIMBALL. *(Mild surprise.)* You know about those?

PATRICK. I've been following them. I'm a bit of a buff. About serial killers. Ed Gein. Ted Bundy. That's what we're dealing with here, isn't it?

DETECTIVE KIMBALL. Yes, but – we're getting close to catching him, Mr. Bateman. We think he's been working for years, but the last few months he's been getting sloppy. Only a matter of time, now.

PATRICK. Good...good luck with that, Detective.

DETECTIVE KIMBALL. Let's be in touch, Mr. Bateman.

[MUSIC NO. 16A "POST-NICE THOUGHT – UNDERSCORE"]

*(***DETECTIVE KIMBALL*** goes. ***PATRICK*** sits at his desk a few moments, contemplates.)*

PATRICK. *(Piecing something together.)* Already this year, there have been four major air disasters, all captured on videotape... The new Oscar de la Renta deodorant I've started to use is giving me a slight rash... The talking ATM on Seventy-Second has started to say things like –

ATM. *(Loud, booming.)* FEED ME A STRAY CAT –

PATRICK. *(To audience.)* Last night, I killed a woman, *not* a prostitute, in my apartment... Am I *trying* to get caught...?

(Turning to door.)

Jean? Jean?

*(**JEAN** enters.)*

What are my next two weeks like, Jean? Can you clear them for me? And get me Evelyn?

JEAN. Of course.

*(**JEAN** goes; a spot on **EVELYN**.)*

EVELYN. *(Answering.)* This is Evelyn.

PATRICK. Evelyn, it's *bone* season; I think we should go away.

EVELYN. *(Flirting.)* Who is this?

PATRICK. It's *Patrick*.

EVELYN. *(Disappointed?)* Oh.

PATRICK. Listen, I need to lay low for a couple of weeks, can we *go* somewhere?

EVELYN. Oh, baby, I wish we could, but ever since I got this stupid promotion –

PATRICK. *(Playing her like a fiddle.)* – Because it feels like we've been losing touch, Evelyn, and I want us to, to reconnect –

[MUSIC NO. 17 "THE END OF AN ISLAND"]

EVELYN. *(Moved by this.)* Oh, honey, in that case, I know *just* the thing: The Hamptons! All of our chums will be there. We'll stay at Tim's. I'll book us a helicopter.

PATRICK. As in, an aircraft?

EVELYN. Oh, Patrick, what would you have us do, rent a *Volvo*?

> *(Sound of a helicopter, racing from New York City to the Hamptons. **EVELYN** and **PATRICK** strip their clothes, revealing summer leisurewear.)*
>
> *(They are joined by **COURTNEY**, **LUIS**, **MCDERMOTT**, **VAN PATTEN**, and various **MALE** and **FEMALE HARDBODIES**; they are sexy and almost naked...)*

EVELYN.	ENSEMBLE.
WE'LL GO FOR A BIKE RIDE	BLAH BLAH BLAH BLAH
WE'LL HEAD TO THE BEACH	BLAH BLAH BLAH BLAH
IF YOU BRING THE PROSECCO,	BLAH BLAH BLAH BLAH
I'LL BRING THE PEACH	BLAH BLAH BLAH BLAH
AND BEHIND THE HEDGES	BLAH DA BLAH DA
THERE DOWN THE LANE	BLAH DA BLAH DA
THEY'RE PLAYING BADMINTON	BLAH DA BLAH DA
IT'S A DANGEROUS GAME	BLAH DA
DANGEROUS GAME	BLAH, BLAH DA, BLAH
WELL EVERYTHING'S GLOWING	OO AH OO AH
ALL IS SUBLIME	OO AH OO AH
AT THE END OF AN ISLAND	OO AH OO AH
IN SUMMERTIME	OO AH OO AH

PATRICK.	
THERE'S ONLY ONE PROBLEM	AH
I'M LOSING MY MIND	AH
AT THE END OF AN ISLAND	AH
IN SUMMERTIME	SUMMERTIME

PATRICK. *(Narrating.)* We jog and go windsurfing; we talk about romantic things like...the moonrise in October over the hills of Virginny...

EVELYN. *Mmm*, Virginny...

PATRICK. We take bubble baths in Tim's big marble tub, go skinny-dipping in the ocean, snuggle under cashmere blankets, but something – is – off... I fantasize about drowning Evelyn in the tub, wrapping her body in the blanket, then dragging it into the surf... (Or did I do that already?)

> *(He and* **EVELYN** *join a party of other, similarly outfitted* **VACATIONERS.**)

EVELYN.	ENSEMBLE.
AT THE GARDEN PARTY	BLAH BLAH BLAH BLAH
MADRASS AND STRIPES	BLAH BLAH BLAH BLAH

PATRICK.

THIS PLACE IS INFESTED	BLAH BLAH BLAH BLAH
WITH FAMILIAR TYPES	BLAH BLAH BLAH BLAH

PATRICK. *(Narrating.)* At night, I roam the beaches, digging up baby crabs under a sky so clear I can see the entire solar system – and the sand dunes, lit by it, seem almost lunar in scale...

EVELYN. Where should we have dinner tonight, darling? Nick and Toni's?

PATRICK. *(To audience and* **EVELYN.***)* This morning, pre-dawn, I microwaved a beached jellyfish and devoured half of it...

EVELYN. *(Not hearing him.)* No, you're right, I am gaining weight out here...

EVELYN & ENSEMBLE.

WELL EVERYTHING'S GLOWING
ALL IS SUBLIME
AT THE END OF AN ISLAND
IN SUMMERTIME

> *(By the end of the song:* **EVELYN,** *in a swimsuit and sunglasses, reclines on a lounge chair, soaking up the sun, napping.* **COURTNEY,** **LUIS, VAN PATTEN,** *and* **MCDERMOTT** *are doing the same.* **PATRICK** *is in swimming trunks, an open shirt, a towel over his shoulder...)*

PATRICK. *(To audience, getting more and more agitated.)* Cut off from New York and my pursuits, I have all the characteristics of a human being (flesh, blood, skin, hair), but my depersonalization is...intensifying. There isn't (I come to accept) a clear, identifiable emotion within me.

(A dread realization.) It was a mistake leaving my natural habitat...

GUYS & GIRLS.
> WE LIKE IT LIKE THIS
> WE'RE TAN AND SMOOTH
> WE SMELL SO GOOD
> THE LOTIONS WE USE

COURTNEY. *(Genuinely curious.)* ...Hey, so I was at the Food Emporium last week...and what, exactly, is the difference between *distilled* and *purified* water? Does anyone know?

VAN PATTEN. With purified water, most of the minerals have been removed. The water has been boiled and the steam has condensed into, *ergo*, purified water.

MCDERMOTT. *Distilled* water, on the other hand, has a flat taste and, usually, it's not for drinking.

COURTNEY. And sparkling water gets its fizz from carbon dioxide, right?

MCDERMOTT, VAN PATTEN & LUIS. Yes!

COURTNEY. I *knew* it!

EVELYN. *(To* **PATRICK,** *flipping through a magazine.)* What are you thinking about, darling?

PATRICK. The body I left back home, in my apartment.

EVELYN. I know, I'm worried about my mail, what if it's piling up?

PATRICK. *(Mind wandering.)* I could take it to the apartment in Hell's Kitchen, the way I did Paul's, but I want to keep the men's bodies separate from the women's, out of respect...

(*To* **EVELYN.***)* You never met Victoria, did you? My neighbor? We kept bumping into each other at the dry cleaners, she'd been sniffing around me for months, so I invited her up to my apartment –

> *(A spot on* **VICTORIA,** *holding a glass of wine, admiring Patrick's Onica.* Everything else is in darkness.)*

---

*Licensees do not have rights to prints by either Man Ray or David Onica and should create original images in the style of these artists.

VICTORIA. Patrick, who hung this painting?

PATRICK. *(Joining her, in the spot.)* I did, Victoria. It's an Onica. Do you like it?

VICTORIA. I do, but Patrick...I'm pretty sure you hung it upside down.

PATRICK. What?

VICTORIA. *(Amused, laughing.)* Yes, you've...hung your Onica upside down. I can't believe that. How funny. Did you do that on purpose?

> *(The lights go back to normal.* **VICTORIA** *exits,* **PATRICK** *goes back to his chair...)*

PATRICK. *(To no one in particular.)* She annoyed me, so I crucified her with a nail gun...

COURTNEY. All right, smart guys, what's the best thing to drink after exercising?

MCDERMOTT. My trainer says Gatorade is good.

VAN PATTEN. Isn't spring water the *best* replacer since it enters the bloodstream faster than any other liquid?

COURTNEY. *(Deep, with meaning.)* I was afraid to try Pellegrino for the first time...but then, once I did, it was fine.

> *(**TIM** pops in.)*

TIM. Guys, wine coolers in the fridge, steaks on the grill, and Whitney on the stereo –

> *(As the others exit:)*

EVELYN. *(Looking at* **PATRICK***, smiling.)* You're just the same, you know? As the boy I met at that mixer in college. I don't know if that's a good thing or a bad thing... Let's say good.

PATRICK. The past isn't real, Evelyn. It's just a dream. Don't mention the past.

EVELYN. What's gotten into you?

PATRICK. I've realized...my need to engage in homicidal behavior on a massive scale...cannot be corrected... Coming out here, I thought...

EVELYN. *(Taking over for him.)* ...I think, Patrick, it would help...if you made a firm commitment.

PATRICK. Maybe. To what?

EVELYN. To us. Our future. Together.

PATRICK. Evelyn, you're missing the essence of what I'm saying: I have a severely impaired capacity to feel.

EVELYN. I know. And what *I'm* saying is: I do, too.

PATRICK. That antique weather vane Tim hung over the fireplace, in there? I'm wondering if I can use it to kill people.

EVELYN. Marry me, Patrick. Let's get married and find out, *together*.

PATRICK. *(To audience.)* "Why not?" I think, suddenly. "Why *not* agree and end up with this girl?

[MUSIC NO. 18 "I AM BACK"]

(Beat.)

(To **EVELYN**.*)* If we can go back to New York, today, this afternoon, in a helicopter –

EVELYN. *(Can hardly believe it.)* Yes, my darling – Anything you want –

PATRICK. *(The simple truth.)* Manhattan protects me.

EVELYN. Then let's get you back there.

(The lights change. **PATRICK** *begins to get dressed, as he did at the top of the show. Careful, highly choreographed movements. If desired or necessary, "***GHOST PAUL***" can help him.)*

PATRICK.

THANK GOD, NEW YORK CITY
THAT LONG ISLAND IS PRETTY SHITTY

BACK TO MY OLD HAUNTS
YOU KNOW MY HEART WANTS WHAT IT WANTS

MAYBE SOME FRESH HELL
AND NO ONE THERE TO KISS AND TELL

A PROSTITUTE, A FRIEND
A MESSY, SATISFYING END

PATRICK.	ENSEMBLE.
NEED I REMIND YOU	AH
OF AN OBVIOUS FACT	
I... AM... BACK!	HE... IS... BACK
DID YOU THINK I WAS AN	AH
AMATEUR	
OR JUST A WEEKEND	
HACK?	
I... AM... BACK!	HE... IS... BACK

(The lights change. Now we're with **PATRICK** *and the two* **PROSTITUTES** *from Act One,* **SABRINA** *and* **CHRISTINE**, *in Paul Owen's apartment.* **PATRICK** *circles them like a shark.)*

PATRICK. *(Turning to them.)* Sabrina. Christine. Hi, ladies, long time.

CHRISTINE. *(Numb, a robot.)* Hi, Paul.

SABRINA. Where have you been, Paul?

PATRICK. I was in London on some business. I'm not really allowed to talk about it, but I can assure you: It was in*credibly* important.

CHRISTINE. This is a new place...

PATRICK. I moved. Do you like it, Christine?

CHRISTINE. It's a palace, compared to the other apartment.

PATRICK. It's not that much nicer.

SABRINA. What'd you do with that painting? The expensive one?

PATRICK. I burned it; it was worthless. Listen, I would *really* like to see the two of you get it on.

(The two **WOMEN** *trade a look.)*

CHRISTINE. *(Wary, unsure.)* But...not like last time?

PATRICK. *(Big smile.)* No, Christine. Nothing like last time.

(Over the course of this song, **PATRICK** *has sex with* **CHRISTINE** *and* **SABRINA**, *then murders*

*and mutilates them both, so that – at the end
– he's using their blood to write a message on
Paul's walls.)*

PATRICK.

I'M READY TO RESTART	
TO EXCAVATE SOME	
BLEEDING HEART	
I'M READY FOR RELEASE	
A LITTLE VIOLENCE TO	
BRING ME PEACE	**ENSEMBLE.**
I'LL TAKE A STRONG	AH
POSITION	
I DON'T HAVE ANY	
INHIBITIONS	
IF YOU WANT TO WATCH	AH
LET ME KNOW	
I'VE GOT IT CAUGHT ON	
VIDEO	
THE LOOK OF FEAR IN	AH
YOUR EYES	
WHEN I ATTACK	
I... AM... BACK!	HE... IS... BACK!

PATRICK, MAN & WOMAN.

AND YOU WILL KNOW	AH
WHEN YOU ARE	AH
STRETCHED UPON	
THE RACK	

PATRICK, 2 MEN & WOMAN.

I... AM... BACK!	HE... IS... BACK!
I WILL HELP YOU SEE	AH
IMPORTANT THINGS YOU	
LACK	
I... AM... BACK!	HE... IS... BACK!
AND YOU WILL SEE A SOUL	AH
THAT'S DARKER STILL	
THAN BLACK	

I... AM... BACK!	HE... IS... BACK!
I... AM... BACK!	HE... IS... BACK!
I... AM... BACK!	HE... IS... BACK!

PATRICK. – I remember – dismember – Sabrina's legs. I use blood from her stumps to scrawl a message across the walls of Paul Owen's apartment – in dripping red letters – something from my memory, from (it seems) a lifetime ago: ABANDON ALL HOPE YE WHO ENTER HERE...

> *(The words – the message – appear in red against the white, filling the stage.)*

> *(The lights change. We shift from Paul's apartment to Barney's. It is crowded with yuppies browsing, shopping the racks.* **PATRICK** *is in a dressing room, getting dressed/ changing –)*

[MUSIC NO. 18 "YOU ARE WHAT YOU WEAR – REPRISE 2"]

ENSEMBLE.
CHANEL, GAULTIER, OR GIORGIO ARMANI
MOSCHINO, ALAÏA, OR NORMA KAMALI
SHOULD WE ROCK THE BETSEY JOHNSON
OR STICK WITH CLASSIC COMME DES GARÇONS

> *(As the blob-like* **ENSEMBLE** *continues to shift and shop,* **LUIS** *approaches.)*

LUIS. Patrick? I didn't know you shopped at this Barney's –

PATRICK. I don't. I'm not here, Luis, goodbye –

> *(**PATRICK** tries to flee;* **LUIS** *catches his arm.)*

LUIS. Wait, Patrick –

> *(Getting close.)*

This whole thing with Evelyn? Marrying her? It's in*sanity.* We can't keep going on like this –

PATRICK. Luis, Get. Your hands. Off of me.

LUIS. Listen, I know you have the same feelings I do, so why – *why* can't we be together?

PATRICK. Luis, you pathetic little faggot – If you do not stop with this "together" bullshit, I *will* slit your fucking throat right here, in Barney's –

LUIS. Please, Patrick – I figured it out: I don't have to marry Courtney, *you* don't have to marry Evelyn, we can relocate to Arizona and buy an inn –

PATRICK. *What the fuck?!*

    (Hang on.)

    – You're marrying Courtney?

LUIS. Not if we go away together –

PATRICK. Oh, my God, Luis, you are, *truly*, the only person *more* insane than I am –

LUIS. I love you, Patrick, *I – love – you –*

PATRICK. I'm *convinced*, Luis – You've *convinced* me – Now have the guts to face reality: I *don't* love you –

    (He shrieks:)

    I – DON'T – LOVE – ANYONE –

    [MUSIC NO. 19A "I DON'T LOVE ANYONE"]

    *(**PATRICK** punches **LUIS** – or bites his face off, though that's confusing –)*

    (– Then crosses to his desk at Pierce and Pierce. He hops on the phone.)

    *(A spot on **COURTNEY**, answering.)*

COURTNEY. Hello, this is Courtney –

PATRICK. *(Emphatic, desperate.)* You *can't* marry Luis!

COURTNEY. *(Beat.)* Why not? You're marrying Evelyn.

PATRICK. That's different!

COURTNEY. What can I say, Patrick? Time is running out for all of us and I want to have children.

PATRICK. But...but...

COURTNEY. But *what*? Only *you* get to be happy?

PATRICK. *– But for the millionth time, Courtney, Luis is a fag!!*

COURTNEY. No, he is *not*, Patrick. Why do you always say that?

PATRICK. *(The ugly truth.)* Because when we were in college, he used to let frat guys tie him up and gang bang him at parties and stuff –

COURTNEY. *(Seriously?)* Oh, my God, Patrick, *college*?

PATRICK. *(Near hysterical.) I'm trying to save your life, you dumb bitch!*

COURTNEY. Oh, well, *that's* nice – Goodbye, Patrick – Do me a favor, *don't* call me again –

> *(She hangs up on **PATRICK**. The lights on her go out as **JEAN** enters Patrick's office –)*

JEAN. *(Worried, she overheard.)* Patrick – is everything all right?

PATRICK. *(No, not at all.)* Jean. Fine. Everything is...fine.

JEAN. You were yelling.

PATRICK. Jean. Jean, Jean, Jean... Would you like to accompany me to dinner, Jean? If you're not...doing anything tonight?

JEAN. Oh! – no. No, I have...no plans.

PATRICK. Well, isn't this a coincidence. Where should we go?

JEAN. I don't know... Doesn't matter.

PATRICK. Come on. Anywhere you want. I can get us in.

JEAN. What about...Dorsia?

PATRICK. *(Beat.)* So-o-o-o-o, Dorsia is where Jean wants to go, Jean's just like everyone else...

JEAN. Oh, I don't care. No, we'll go wherever you want.

PATRICK. No, no. If Dorsia is what you want, Dorsia is what you – deserve...

But, uh. Why don't we meet at my place for a drink beforehand? Would you like that?

JEAN. Yes. S-sure. If you don't think Evelyn –

PATRICK. *(Cutting her off, sharp.)* Jean, you don't have anyone visiting you right now, do you? Staying with you? Your sister?

JEAN. No. It's just me.

PATRICK. *(What is he planning?)* Perfect.

[MUSIC NO. 20 "A GIRL BEFORE"]

See you at my place, then. Take the rest of the day. Go home, get changed. Wear something, I don't know, special. Let's make this a special night.

JEAN. Okay...

> *(The lights shift.* **JEAN** *starts getting ready for her date with* **PATRICK** *– who starts getting ready for his date with Jean. Needless to say, they have very different expectations for how the evening is going to play out...)*

HE DOESN'T SOUND ALL RIGHT
HIS VOICE A LITTLE THIN
DOES HE NEED SOMEONE
THE WAY THAT I NEED HIM

DOES EVERYTHING HE HAS AMOUNT TO ENOUGH
DOES HE NEED SOMEONE TO HOLD
WHEN IT GETS ROUGH

AM I SOMEONE HE COULD LINGER ON?
OR WOULD HE SIMPLY MOVE ALONG
AM I SOMEONE HE WOULD LOVE MORE
WOULD I BE JUST A GIRL BEFORE
A GIRL BEFORE
A GIRL BEFORE

> *(***JEAN*** *has slipped into a beautiful dress. As she sings, she dances with the* **PATRICK** *of her dreams...)*

HE LOOKS AT ME SOMETIMES
IN A CERTAIN WAY
ALL THE FEARS I HAVE
SEEM TO FADE AWAY

I KNOW THAT I'M A FOOL
TO THINK THAT THIS IS REAL
I'M BREAKING EVERY RULE
'CAUSE THIS IS HOW I FEEL

AM I SOMEONE HE COULD LINGER ON?
OR WOULD HE SIMPLY MOVE ALONG
AM I SOMEONE HE WOULD LOVE MORE
WOULD I BE JUST A GIRL BEFORE
A GIRL BEFORE
A GIRL BEFORE

> *(The song ends.* **JEAN** *is now sitting in Patrick's apartment, on his couch.* **PATRICK** *is puttering around, messing with a roll of duct tape – but nothing more obvious than that – nothing to break the spell...)*

...I'd like to travel – maybe go back to school, I don't really know... I'm at a point in my life where there seems to be a lot of possibilities, but I'm so...

(She notices him staring at her.) ...What? Did I say something wrong?

PATRICK. No. No, it's just – what you just said. About possibilities...reminded me of a girl I knew in college once.

JEAN. First love?

> *(Awkward beat.)*

Anyway, I'm a bit unsure about the future.

PATRICK. I just want to have a meaningful relationship with somebody unique, you know?

JEAN. That makes sense.

PATRICK. To live happily ever after, right? *That's* what he wants –

> *(Catching himself.)*

– *I* want.

JEAN. That's why people need each other, I guess. To be happy.

PATRICK. Some don't. Or, well, people adjust to their circumstances.

JEAN. You're not one of those people, Patrick. You're –

(JEAN keeps talking, but we don't hear her, just PATRICK, in a tight, sharp spot. His inner monologue.)

PATRICK. Oh, Jean. Where *you* see nature and earth, life and water, *I* see an unending desert landscape, devoid of reason, and light, and spirit –

(Back to "normal.")

JEAN. – But, I mean, haven't you ever wanted to make someone happy?

PATRICK. *(Trying to refocus.)* ...What? What was that?

JEAN. Haven't you ever wanted to make someone happy? Evelyn? Or someone else?

(Beat, no, then:)

PATRICK. Did you know, Jean, that Ted Bundy's first dog, a collie, was named Lassie? Had you heard that?

JEAN. Who's Ted Bundy?

PATRICK. Forget it – you were saying?

JEAN. Oh, nothing, just that...

(Beat; she goes for it:)

I think I'm in love with you, Patrick.

(Everything stops for a moment. Then:)

PATRICK. ...*Why?*

JEAN. Well, because you're...concerned with others, and that's a rare thing in what, I guess, is a hedonistic world.

(Beat.)

PATRICK. What else?

JEAN. You're...sweet, and sweetness is...sexy. As is mystery, and I think...you're mysterious. And I think...shy men are romantic...

(PATRICK's dead quiet, silent.)

Patrick? Talk to me?

PATRICK. *(He looks at her, makes a decision.)* ...I think... I think...you should leave, Jean. I think you should go home...

JEAN. *(Mortified.)* Oh, no. Did I ruin it by telling you?

PATRICK. No... Don't be scared, but...if you stayed, I think I might hurt you...

JEAN. You couldn't –

PATRICK. I don't think I could control myself... You, you don't want to be hurt, do you?

JEAN. No.

> *(Reaching for him.)*

> Patrick –

PATRICK. *(Stepping back from her, saying simply:)* The truth is...I've never wanted to make anyone happy, not even myself.

JEAN. *(A shock; does she believe him?)* Patrick...

PATRICK. *(Quietly, plaintively.)* Get out, Jean, please.

> *(She doesn't move; he roars:)*

– GO!!

[MUSIC NO. 21A "CONFESSION"]

> *(She goes.* **PATRICK** *is alone. He takes a business card out of his jacket pocket, goes to his phone, dials a number. As it rings:)*

(To audience.) There is an idea of Patrick Bateman, some kind of abstraction, but there is no *real* me, only an entity, *this* entity –

(Into phone.) Hello, Detective Kimball? Patrick Bateman, you came to see me about Paul Owen's disappearance?

(To audience.) And though you can shake my hand, and feel my flesh gripping yours, *I simply am not there* –

(Into phone.) I killed Paul Owen with an axe, Detective. And not just Paul.

Dozens and dozens of people, too many to count, most of them women, you can't imagine –

PATRICK. *(To audience.)* The truth is, it is hard for me to make sense on *any* given level. I am fabricated, an aberration – *(Into phone.)* I can tell you where all the bodies are, Detective, I keep some of them in an apartment in Hell's Kitchen, but lately, I've been using, you'll appreciate this, Paul Owen's apartment as a, a meat locker –

(To audience.) My conscience, my pity, my hopes disappeared a long time ago (probably at Harvard), if they ever existed. There are no more barriers to cross, no more frontiers, I am without limit, and – and –

(Into phone.) – And I'm a pretty sick guy, Detective, and I almost hurt someone...*good*... So I think you may have to stop me, or something...when you get this message...

    (Beep!)

PATRICK.

NOW I'M CLEAN
I'VE BECOME CLEAN
THE THINGS I'VE SEEN
STILL I'M CLEAN

ENSEMBLE.

CLEAN, BECOME CLEAN
OH SO CLEAN
NOW HE'S CLEAN, SO
    CLEAN
CLEAN, CLEAN, CLEAN
ALL OF THE THINGS HE'S
    SEEN
WHAT HE'S SEEN, WHERE
    HE'S BEEN
HE'S A LIVING DREAM
DREAM, DREAM
NOW WE'RE CLEAN
DREAM YOUR DREAM
BE CLEAN, CLEAN
DREAM YOUR DREAM
WE NOW ARE CLEAN

(The lights shift; **PATRICK** *crosses to Pierce and Pierce. The next morning. Post-date awkwardness with* **JEAN***:)*

JEAN. Good morning, Patrick. How are you?

PATRICK. *(At peace?)* Slept like a baby, Jean. No dreams, no – nightmares. I'm ready for – whatever's next.

JEAN. *(Nervous as hell.)* Patrick...I hope you're not disappointed in me about last night. For admitting my feelings towards you.

PATRICK. No. Not at all, Jean. I found your confession... inspiring, in fact.

JEAN. ...Good, I'm glad.

PATRICK. I'm calling HR this a.m., Jean. You're getting a promotion. You deserve it, for putting up with all my bullshit. Also: A better benefits package, I want you taken care of.

JEAN. *(Holy shit!)* Patrick...I, I don't know what to say...

PATRICK. Just say "Yes," Jean.

JEAN. *(She smiles.) Yes.*

PATRICK. Thank you, Jean. For everything.

*(***JEAN*** exits, ***TIM*** enters.)*

TIM. Bateman!

PATRICK. *(Startled.)* Fuck! Jesus...

TIM. Whoa. *You're* on edge.

PATRICK. – Sorry, I'm...waiting for a shoe to drop.

TIM. It already did. They're gonna announce it at the partners meeting tomorrow.

PATRICK. Announce what?

TIM. Oh, nada mucho. Just that you're getting the Fisher account.

PATRICK. ...Wha...what? ...I am?

TIM. Effective immediately, you'll be the one taking it to the next level – By the way, I wasn't supposed to say anything, so – act surprised when they tell you, okay?

PATRICK. I will... I am...

TIM. Hey, we should celebrate. The inner circle. Get the whole sick crew together. Whattya say, pal – Tunnel? For old times' sake?

> (*The lights change. We're in Tunnel. Everyone rocking out, as our gang –* **MCDERMOTT, VAN PATTEN, TIM, LUIS, EVELYN, COURTNEY, SEAN,** *and* **PATRICK** *– gathers.*)
>
> **[MUSIC NO. 22 "DON'T YOU WANT ME"]***
>
> [**PAUL, LUIS, SEAN,** *and* **ENSEMBLE** *sing "Don't You Want Me."*]
>
> (*The music becomes underscoring as the scene takes over...*)

EVELYN. The timing of this couldn't be more perfect, Timothy, what with the wedding almost upon us – oh, oh which reminds me: Patrick and I would love, love, *love*, for you to be our best man –

PATRICK. – Could we – can we talk about something *relevant*, please?

LUIS. What did you have in mind – *Bateman*?

PATRICK. I don't know, *Carruthers*, like: Where do we have reservations?

COURTNEY. God, Patrick, when did you become such a control freak?

PATRICK. Sorry, I just always feel better when I know where I'm going next – What about 220? McDermott, check the Zagat's –

MCDERMOTT. No fucking way. The coke I scored there last time was cut with so much laxative I had to –

VAN PATTEN. Ee-NUFF! Jesus, low point of the night much?

SEAN. I can call Dorsia and get us in.

EVELYN. Oh-la-la, Dorsia. My goodness!

PATRICK. I *highly* doubt that, Sean.

---

*Licensees should refer to their piano/conductor books for the lyrics to Music No. 22 "Don't You Want Me."

SEAN. The maître d' was one of my roommates freshman year, you ass. Deal with it. Should I call?

EVERYONE BUT PATRICK. – *YES!!*

(**PATRICK***'s distracted by something, silent.*)

EVELYN. Patrick? Is Dorsia all right?

TIM. Come on, Bateman. We're waiting –

PATRICK. I'm sorry, will you excuse me...?

(**PATRICK** *is looking at the bar, where* **DETECTIVE KIMBALL** *sits, by himself, nursing a drink.*)

...I, I have to return some videotapes.

(*As* **PATRICK** *goes,* **EVELYN** *calls out to him:*)

EVELYN. *Patrick! It's Dorsia! We're* going*!*

(*But* **PATRICK** *is with* **DETECTIVE KIMBALL** *now. A spot on them; everything else is dark.*)

PATRICK. Detective Kimball?

DETECTIVE KIMBALL. Mr. Bateman. How are you? Having a night out?

PATRICK. I am, yes. I'm a-rocking and a-rolling. But, uh. I've been thinking I might hear from you...

DETECTIVE KIMBALL. About?

(*Awkward beat.*)

PATRICK. Well, I mean...did you get my message? The one I left you, the sort of...*rambling* confession?

DETECTIVE KIMBALL. Oh! God, yes. That was – So that *was* you? Oh, Mr. Bateman, I have to tell you, that was hilarious. You killing Paul Owen, and the escort girls, and all the others, that was – brilliant. You're a very talented man, Mr. Bateman. You should be an actor.

PATRICK. Detective...

(*Deeply confused.*)

...you don't seem to understand. That whole message I left you?

DETECTIVE KIMBALL. Yes?

PATRICK. Was true. I tortured and killed – dozens of people. I killed Paul Owen and chopped him up. And, also...*I liked it. A lot.* I really – I can't be any clearer than that.

DETECTIVE KIMBALL. Mr. Bateman, that's just not possible.

PATRICK. *(Almost existential.)* Why? *Why* isn't it possible?

DETECTIVE KIMBALL. Because I had *dinner* with Paul Owen, in London, where he is, indeed, hiding out.

PATRICK. *(Quiet shock.)* What?

[MUSIC NO. 22A "DETECTIVE KIMBALL"]

DETECTIVE KIMBALL. I found him and had dinner with him. *(Actually.)* Twice, in fact.

PATRICK. And he was, like, *alive*?

DETECTIVE KIMBALL. Oh, very much so. And mortified about the whole thing. Apologized for wasting my time. Bought me tickets to *Les Miz* on the West End. *Excellent* show, by the way, if you haven't seen it.

PATRICK. But...but...

(Trying a different tack.) Okay, what about the escort girls? Did you go to Paul Owen's apartment? Did you see their bodies? The blood on the walls?

DETECTIVE KIMBALL. I *have* been to Paul Owen's apartment, Mr. Bateman, just today, in fact – have *you*?

> (**PATRICK** *is completely perplexed, standing there, in the bar. He crosses the stage to Paul Owen's apartment – now a blinding white space. The whole stage, everything's white, immaculate, untouched, like a virgin field of snow.*)

MRS. WOLFE. *(To* **PATRICK.***)* I'm Mrs. Wolfe, the real estate agent, can I help you?

PATRICK. I'm looking for... Doesn't Paul Owen live here?

> (**MRS. WOLFE** *stares at* **PATRICK** *for a long time before answering him.*)

MRS. WOLFE. No. He doesn't, in fact.

PATRICK. Are you, like, *sure* about that?

MRS. WOLFE. *(Smiling.)* You saw the ad for the apartment? In the *Times*?

PATRICK. No... I mean, *yes*, yes, I did, in the *Times*... But I think Paul Owen still owns this place.

MRS. WOLFE. *(Chilling pause.)* There was no ad in the *Times*.

    (Beat.)

So I think you should go.

PATRICK. *(Breathless.)* What happened here? With the bodies, the blood? On the walls?

MRS. WOLFE. Don't make any trouble.

PATRICK. *(The abyss.)* This isn't a game, this is my life.

MRS. WOLFE. I suggest you go.

PATRICK. But...

MRS. WOLFE. Don't make any trouble.

PATRICK. I...

MRS. WOLFE. And don't ever come back here.

PATRICK. ...I won't. Don't worry.

    *(**PATRICK** backs away from **MRS. WOLFE**, stunned. She exits, leaving him alone.)*

    (Then he takes a beat, and it's as if he's realized he's been performing in front of an audience all night long.)

[MUSIC NO. 23 "THIS IS NOT AN EXIT"]

    *(**PATRICK** addresses the audience, witnesses to his crimes, directly, purposefully.)*

MAYBE THIS SCHISM
IS JUST A SYMPTOM
OF LATE CAPITALISM
OF SAVIORS DIED AND RISEN
OF WORLDS THAT WOULDN'T LISTEN
TO THEIR OWN COLLAPSE

    *(**PATRICK** starts to undress and dress one last time. From the suit he's wearing into...the coat and tails of a society groom.)*

PATRICK.
EVEN IF THIS STORY
SEEMS OVERWROUGHT AND GORY
IT'S NOT A FABLE
NOT AN ALLEGORY
NO CAUTIONARY TALE
NO MEMENTO MORI
OR A VAGUE PERHAPS
MAYBE YOU'VE BEEN SLAUGHTERED
MAYBE YOU'VE BEEN KISSED
EITHER WAY MEANS NOTHING
I SIMPLY DON'T EXIST
LOOK AT WHAT'S BEEN DONE HERE
AND JUDGE IT HOW YOU WISH
I AM ALL ALONE HERE
I AM THE SOLIPSIST

THIS IS WHAT WE'VE COME TO
WHAT WE HAVE BECOME
I AM NOT A PERSON
KNOWN TO ANYONE
ALL THE DOORS ARE TRIED AND TESTED
KNOW THAT THIS IS NOT AN EXIT

> (**EVELYN**, *in a beautiful wedding gown, enters, slowly processing toward* **PATRICK**, *her husband-to-be.*)

AM I JUST A VERSION
OF THE END OF DAYS?
AM I JUST AN EFFECT
OF A MODERN PHASE?
AM I JUST THE END POINT
OF THE GRAND PARADE?
SHOULD WE BE AFRAID?

> (*Patrick's guests – the living and the dead, including* **PAUL, CHRISTINE, SABRINA, VICTORIA** *– gather around* **PATRICK** *and* **EVELYN**. **COURTNEY** *is Evelyn's maid of honor; Patrick's* **MOTHER** *is there, in her sunglasses.* **SEAN***'s the best man.*)

(The **ENSEMBLE** *joins* **PATRICK** *in song:)*

PATRICK & PAUL.	ENSEMBLE.
MAYBE YOU'VE BEEN SLAUGHTERED	MAYBE
MAYBE YOU'VE BEEN KISSED	
EITHER WAY MEANS NOTHING	MAYBE
I SIMPLY DON'T EXIST	
LOOK AT WHAT'S BEEN DONE HERE	NOTHING
JUDGE IT HOW YOU WISH	
I AM ALL ALONE HERE	ALL
I AM THE SOLIPSIST	ALONE
THIS IS WHAT WE'VE COME TO	MAYBE
WHAT WE HAVE BECOME	MAYBE
I AM NOT A PERSON	
KNOWN TO ANYONE	ALL
ALL THE DOORS ARE TRIED AND TESTED	THE DOORS ARE
KNOW THAT THIS IS NOT AN EXIT	TRIED AND TESTED

(PATRICK *and* **EVELYN** *are wed.)*

NONE OF THIS	NONE OF THIS
EXISTS FOR ME	EXISTS
THIS IS ALL A FANTASY	NONE OF THIS
THERE IS NO FUTURE HERE	EXISTS
THERE IS NO HISTORY	NONE OF
NONE OF THIS IS REAL	THIS
IT'S NOT REALITY	IS REAL
NONE OF THIS	NONE OF THIS
EXISTS FOR ME	EXISTS
THERE IS NO CONSISTENCY	NONE OF THIS
THERE IS ONLY ENTROPY	EXISTS
AND EVEN THOUGH I'VE TRIED AND TESTED	TRIED AND TESTED
I KNOW THAT THIS IS NOT AN EXIT NOW...	NOT AN EXIT NOW

(The song is playing out; we end as we began, with **PATRICK** *alone. He is in a spot, surrounded by darkness.)*

PATRICK. I am twenty-seven years old, living in New York City at the end of the century, and *this* is what being Patrick Bateman means to me...

(Full, quick blackout.)

End of Show